Other Works by This Author

As T. Kingfisher

Nine Goblins (Goblinhome Book 1)
Toad Words and Other Stories
Bryony and Roses

As Ursula Vernon

Black Dogs Duology
House of Diamond
Mountain of Iron
It Made Sense at the Time

Digger Series
Digger (Omnibus Edition)

For Children

Hamster Princess: Harriet the Invincible

Castle Hangnail

*Nurk: The Strange, Surprising Adventures
of a (Somewhat) Brave Shrew*

Comics Squad: Recess!

Dragonbreath Series

THE
SEVENTH
BRIDE

THE
SEVENTH
BRIDE

T. KINGFISHER

Text copyright © 2015 Ursula Vernon

Published by 47North, Seattle

www.apub.com

Amazon, the Amazon logo, and 47North are trademarks of Amazon.com, Inc., or its affiliates.

ISBN-13: 9781503949751
ISBN-10: 1503949753

Cover illustrated by Levi Pinfold

Cover design by Jason Blackburn

Printed in the United States of America

For Brooke
(stone)

Chapter One

Her name was Rhea.

Her father said that she had been named after a great and powerful goddess of the old days, the queen of all the gods, but in that country at that time, there weren't many books about gods. There were too many problems with wizards and fairies and odd things popping up in the corners of the potato field for anyone to want to invite more supernatural intervention. People prayed, when they prayed at all, to the old saints and heroes of the country—Saint Olio and Cullan the Archer and the Lady of Stones, saints who might be expected to understand the special trials of living in that land—and left the gods alone.

As a result, when Rhea tried to look up anything related to "rhea" in the few books available to a miller's daughter, all she could find were pictures of a probably mythical creature that looked like a giant, ill-tempered chicken with a very long neck. There was no reason that a goddess had to look human, of course—plenty of them had never been human, which was part of the reason that the saints were safer—but if an immortal had to pick a shape, a giant long-necked chicken seemed like an odd choice.

Rhea the girl felt that, had she been Rhea the goddess, she would have done a better job there. There were plenty of lovely and noble birds, like eagles and peacocks and phoenixes, which would have been a vast improvement over the rhea.

Probably not swans, though. With their high, proud necks and dark eyes, swans were beautiful, but if you saw one while you were sitting on the stream bank, enjoying a bit of lunch, you had better run. They hissed like serpents, and those beautiful white wings could hit like a sledgehammer.

(And there was nothing quite like turning up at home, beaten and bloody and bruised, and having to explain that you'd been abused up one side of the lawn and down the other by a limpid-eyed waterfowl.)

Rhea had learned at a young age to beat a hasty retreat from swans.

On the other hand, she had to admit that she had never met an eagle or a peacock or a phoenix, either, and it was entirely possible that they were just as obnoxious as swans. Rhea was not notably more cynical than the average fifteen-year-old, but she thought that this was likely. She did not know many beautiful animals that had sweet tempers, except perhaps butterflies. Then again, there wasn't enough to a butterfly to properly be called a temper. What options did an angry butterfly have, anyway? Stamping eyelash-sized feet? Flapping its wings in a sarcastic manner?

In that regard, Rhea thought glumly, they weren't much different from millers' daughters. She could slam doors and drag her feet and feed the chickens in as furious a fashion as possible, but her anger was no more effective than a butterfly's. No one was going to listen.

She was fifteen years old, and engaged.

That was more than enough to be angry about.

Sure, some girls did get married that young. Even younger, sometimes, but not often. Long ago, girls had married at twelve and thirteen, but that had been in the bad old days when there was plague about, and if you didn't marry young, you might not live to marry at all. Nobody did that now—or rather, girls who got married at that age still lived at home, and they didn't properly become wives for years and years. Such arrangements usually involved dowries and politics and, sometimes, lords and ladies.

Anyway, the point was, they weren't really married. They were just kids who'd gotten some paperwork out of the way. Generally, if you married for real at fifteen, it was because you had been doing something improper and your parents were determined that the young man do The Honorable Thing.

Rhea certainly couldn't be accused of that. There weren't even any boys she liked. And yet here she was with a silver band on her finger.

Lord Crevan hadn't set a date yet. That was something. Quite a lot, actually. The notice of engagement had been posted on the meeting hall door, but she might not be expected to actually stand before the priest with him for quite some time.

That helped.

The meeting hall door was black oak and had once been carved with fantastic monsters, all three-headed wolves and griffins and dragons and elephants. (No rheas. She'd looked.) At one time, it had been a masterpiece. Unfortunately, that had been about two centuries prior, and so many notices and wedding banns and wanted posters had been stuck there over the years that the monsters were full of nail holes.

She'd always assumed that someday there'd be a notice nailed to the wolf's middle forehead about her engagement. Just not yet.

Marriage was like death. You knew it'd happen eventually, but it wasn't something to dwell on.

Mind you, a miller's daughter could do a lot worse than a wealthy minor noble, particularly a miller's daughter of no particular beauty and a less-than-thorough mastery of the domestic arts.

And Lord Crevan had been very understanding about her being so young. He had left her a gift, a dress dyed in a spectacular shade of red, the sort of dress a lady wore in her manor house—not at all the kind a miller's daughter wore. If you tried to wear a red dress in a room filled with flour, it would be dusty pink by the end of the day. Her aunt had suffered heart palpitations at the sight of it and had to go have a lie-down.

She still didn't know what to think about the dress. It had never occurred to her to even dream about a dress like that. She was almost afraid to touch it.

Really, Crevan was an ideal suitor.

She hadn't expected to love her husband. That sort of thing almost never happened outside ballads anyway, so that wasn't what bothered her. She'd been raised with the understanding that you married well and you were polite to each other, and if you were lucky, you became relatively good friends, because after all, you were both stuck in this together. That was all she'd ever hoped for.

It was just . . . just . . .

Something nagged at the back of her brain, a niggling little itch, as if she had a mosquito bite on the inside of her skull. It was like a whisper, just below what she could quite hear, and what it was whispering was "Something isn't quite right here. Something is going on . . ."

I wonder what it is . . .

Chapter Two

A week earlier, her father had informed her of Lord Crevan's intentions by listing the facts in order of importance.

"He's very rich," her father had said. "He's a noble. And he's interested in you."

Rhea had been sitting on the wobbly stool in the kitchen, rocking back and forth and enjoying the slightly uneasy sensation as the short leg went thunk against the floor. When her father got to the last bit, she was in midwobble, forgot to catch herself, and nearly fell sideways onto the cat.

"*What?*"

"He wants to make an offer for you," her father said patiently.

For a rather absurd moment, all Rhea could think of was that he wanted to buy her like he would buy a horse or a sack of flour, and she wondered how much she'd be worth.

Quite a bit more than a sack of flour. Probably not as much as a good horse. Several goats at least, I should think. "Wait—*what?*"

"He wants to marry you," said her mother gently from where she was stirring the soup.

"Marry me?"

"This is going to take a while," her aunt muttered, punctuating each word with the chop of a knife on the cutting board.

"You all knew about this?" Rhea asked, rising to her feet. She wasn't sure which was more infuriating, that some stranger was interested in marrying her or that her whole family had apparently known about it without immediately telling her.

At the moment, the second one was the only thing she could focus on. Marriage was so far from her thoughts that it was like some far-off foreign country, possibly with elephants.

"A noble?"

"He's a friend of the viscount's," said her father. "He has lands . . . well, I'm not quite sure where. I think he has a hunting lodge nearby."

Rhea tried to absorb this and failed utterly. "But you knew about this?" she said to her mother.

"Do you not want to get married, then?" asked her mother.

"No!" And then, when the blatant untruth of that hung in the air, "Well . . . eventually. I hadn't much thought about it."

"Well, why don't you take a few days to think about it?" said her mother, still in that gentle, implacable voice.

Which meant "Take a few days to resign yourself."

Which meant "We don't have a choice."

It wasn't fair when her mother used that voice. Trying to resist it was like trying to kick a blizzard.

"But—"

"Just think. You'll have a whole house to yourself . . . and servants," put in her aunt.

Rhea looked at her father, hoping for a reprieve.

He seemed exhausted, and his mask of enthusiasm was strained around the edges. "Rhea—sweetheart—you know that it's been harder to make the rents lately . . ."

Faced with this united front, Rhea did the only thing she could think to do, which was to storm out of the cottage and slam the door behind her.

It would have been a lot easier if her parents had been wicked, she thought later.

It wasn't that she particularly *wanted* to be fattened up and eaten, or turned into a donkey, or forced to wear hair shirts and ashes like the children of wicked parents in fairy tales. But if your parents were wicked, you needn't worry about pleasing them. When they were doing the best they could, you had no traction at all.

She sat under the stairs at the mill and brooded.

It was a good spot. You could watch the stream from between the steps, but you were unlikely to attract the attention of any passing swans.

Mills are full of grinding gears and grinding grain, so they tend to vibrate a great deal. It took two separate foundations to keep the mill from shaking itself apart. So the cottage where Rhea lived with her parents and her aunt was not attached to the mill. It lay on the other side of a broad field, a little ways upstream. If she leaned out sideways and craned her neck, she could just see it.

Their home was a large, neatly kept cottage, with a well-tended yard full of chickens. Hollyhocks grew along the side, in shades of red and violet, unless magic had gotten into them again, in which case they had a tendency to go plaid.

Rhea loved living there. She hadn't realized that, not until her aunt had said she would have a whole house to herself when she became Lord Crevan's wife. The prospect of losing the cottage had never occurred to her before.

She was surprised by how much it hurt.

Sure, her aunt was a skinflint and could be grumpy, and sure, Rhea's bedroom under the eaves echoed with the sounds of her dad snoring downstairs at night. Yes, wind crept through the chinks in the wall, particularly in winter, and small crawling things were always falling out of the thatch and onto the head of anyone unlucky enough to be standing under them. But it was *her* house.

She knew all the tricks. She knew which rung of the ladder shifted under her feet, which boards creaked, and where the hot spots were in the oven if you were baking bread. She knew where the damp spots in the garden were that attracted slugs, the dry spots where plants needed a little extra water to get them through the summers, and the place where you didn't plant hollyhocks or, saints forbid, rutabagas.

Having a new home—even if she was the lady of it—sounded depressing.

She brooded some more.

Movement caught her eye, and she looked up.

It was her mother, coming down the streamside path. Her face was pink, as it always was when she'd been cooking.

"Rhea? Dinner's ready."

"I'm not hungry," Rhea said, which was mostly a lie.

"Uh-huh."

Her mother stood by the stairs without saying anything. After a minute, it became obvious she wasn't going anywhere, and Rhea crawled out from behind the steps.

"It won't be that bad," her mother said as they walked back up the path.

"How do *you* know?"

Her tone was surly, but her mother laughed, which surprised her. "Do you think I was never young? I'd hardly met your father when our parents arranged for us to wed. I cried for three days beforehand. It worked out well enough for us."

Rhea blinked. Her mother had never mentioned this before. It was hard to imagine her parents that young, and her mother crying for days over the prospect of marrying her father.

Still—

"I've never even *seen* him," she said, aggrieved. "How does he even know I exist?"

"Well," said her mother, "that, at least, will be remedied. He told your father that he would come by in a few days for your answer."

Rhea kicked a pebble on the path and watched it bounce into the grass. The fact that her mother hadn't answered her question did not escape her. "So I can still say no?"

There was a long silence from her mother.

"Honey . . ."

The gentle tone was all Rhea needed. She wiped at her face and found, to her immense annoyance, that there were tears.

"We don't want you to be unhappy," said her mother. "Not for the world. And you'll be marrying above your station, much better than we ever hoped, and that's a good thing, a *wonderful* thing—"

Rhea pinched the bridge of her nose. "Yes. I know. Aunt was very clear."

Her mother sighed. "It's been a hard patch for everyone," she said. "And if the farmers don't have grain, we can't grind it. The viscount's been very good—very understanding—and we need him to keep being understanding. Marrying a friend of his . . ."

She trailed off, but Rhea could fill in the silence well enough on her own.

"But why me? Why not someone older or better or, or . . . *prettier*?"

At this point, Rhea's mother should have said, "You're as pretty as anyone," or some variation on that theme. It was part of the job of mothers to assure their offspring that they were beautiful and worthy and that it wasn't surprising that anyone would want them.

Instead, her mother said, "I don't know."

And that was the most alarming thing of all.

Chapter Three

Rhea finally met Lord Crevan four days later, when she was lying in wait for the swan.

There was only one that claimed this stretch of the millrace. A bare patch over one eye gave it a perpetual glare, and its elegant neck arched over the heart of a born bully.

Each day, it came for her lunch.

Rhea couldn't eat her lunch anywhere in the mill—she had tried, and the vibrations made her dreadfully queasy—but neither could she leave the building unattended. The morning's grain had already been dropped off and recorded. As was usually the case lately, there hadn't been much, so her parents were away, trying to make up the shortfall with odd jobs elsewhere.

Still, someone had to stay at the mill in case one of the hoppers jammed.

This left her entirely at the mercy of the swan.

Rhea had learned everything she knew about hate from her encounters with this swan.

A large clump of cattails grew downstream from the millrace, and Rhea lurked behind it. Sharp leaves pricked through her clothes and left thin scrapes along her arms, but she didn't care.

She wore breeches since flowing fabric was dangerous around all the machinery in the mill, a tightly belted tunic, and a light dusting of flour. The flour turned her coppery skin a muted clay color and made her black hair prematurely gray, but she didn't care about that, either.

Today, she would finally have her revenge.

A flash of white glinted through the reeds. A moment later, there was a splash.

Rhea brandished her instrument of vengeance, and sank lower behind the reeds.

With a hiss, the swan waddled into view. It caught sight of her and spread its wings, like a cobra spreading its hood.

Rhea rose to face it.

"Last chance," she told the swan. "Last chance to call it quits, bird." She felt positively dangerous. The fact that she'd sunk ankle deep in the mud and her toes were getting soggy barely registered.

The swan eyed her. Somewhere in its tiny, savage brain, it knew that she wasn't acting normally. They had a ritual, after all: It went for her lunch, and she screamed and ran away. Then it pecked the lunch out of her hands, taking as much skin with it as possible, and whacked her with a wing if she tried to retaliate.

That was how this was supposed to go. They had refined it to an art.

She wasn't supposed to stand her ground and make noises.

It hissed uncertainly.

"I don't want to do this," Rhea said. The sandwich seemed to burn in her hands.

It took another step forward, then two. Its eyes locked onto the sandwich.

"On your beak be it!"

And she hurled the sandwich at the bird. The *special* sandwich. The sandwich that she had spent yesterday evening carefully hollowing out so as to accommodate the largest horse turd she could find.

The swan snapped it out of the air and began gulping it down as rapidly as possible.

Rhea leaned forward.

Just when she was afraid that the swan's appetite had defeated her best efforts, the bird slowed down.

It kept eating for a moment or two, apparently out of sheer disbelief, while green bits dropped from the sides of its beak. Olive streaks drooled down the luxurious white feathers. The swan hissed again, awkwardly, and began shaking its head. Bread crumbs sprayed. Rhea stepped back.

The swan's wings drooped. It dropped its head and began frantically wiping the sides of its bill along the grass.

"That'll teach you," said Rhea with deep satisfaction.

The swan turned and waddled away. It staggered into the millstream, dipped its head underwater, and made odd snorting sounds one didn't usually associate with swans.

"Humph." Rhea dusted off her hands as the gargling swan swept away out of sight.

She hadn't wanted to hurt the swan. Sure, she could have laid hands on a pitchfork or a reaping scythe easily enough, but it wasn't in her nature. She even cringed when her mother killed a chicken for dinner.

Something had snapped the other day, though. She couldn't do anything about Lord Crevan, she couldn't do anything about getting married, she couldn't do anything about being fifteen, but two days ago, when the swan had snagged her lunch, she'd realized that here was *something* she could do.

And she'd done it.

She probably couldn't get out of marriage by feeding Crevan a horse manure sandwich. Maybe there were other options.

She turned away from the stream, her head held high as she pulled out her sandwich.

When she caught a flash of white out of the corner of her eye, her first thought was of her enemy. Certain that the swan was mounting a treacherous rear assault, she bolted to her feet, sandwich held high over her head, ready to break and run.

The man in white cleared his throat.

"You're not a swan," she said.

He raised both eyebrows. "I've been accused of many things, but never that."

He wore a flowing white shirt, which had caught Rhea's eye, and a long, sweeping blue cloak. His boots were pointed and had elegantly cut cuffs. They were not boots that had ever stomped around a farmyard. His hair and skin were as dark as Rhea's own, but considerably better groomed.

Behind him, reins thrown carelessly over its neck, stood a large horse. Its coat shone the almost pink of strawberry roan, and its hooves were the size of dinner plates. Rhea realized that she must have been very intent on her vengeance on the swan not to have heard the approaching hoofbeats.

Oh, hell, thought Rhea, *I've just insulted a noble. If "you're not a swan" is really an insult, which I'm not sure about.*

"Errr," she said, "sorry . . . I wasn't expecting . . . ," she began, and then realized she was very close to babbling and clamped her teeth together.

"Neither was I," he said agreeably. "I am Lord Crevan."

Ah. Yes. Of course. She felt very stupid for not having guessed, but of course the odds of *two* nobles stopping by to talk to her were, well, actually not that much lower than the odds of *one* noble stopping by to talk to her—and here he was, and dear god, he was *old*. He was at least as old as her father, and she didn't *want* to marry him and—

Easy. First things first. Don't just stand here and stare at him as if he were a viper.

She dropped to a curtsy, remembered too late that she was wearing breeches, and had to make do. *Damn.*

"I'm Rhea. The, uh, miller's daughter. Milord." *Soon to be your fiancée, but I won't be the one to mention that.*

"A pleasure to meet you," he said, inclining his head. "I've been watching you for some time. It is good to speak to you at last."

He's been watching me?

Rhea wasn't sure what bothered her more, that a strange man had been watching her or that he was perfectly willing to admit it.

As if I wouldn't object to someone watching me!

They stood in awkward silence for a moment. Rhea's hands were sweating, and she tried to rub them unobtrusively on the sides of her legs. He was studying her closely, and she was acutely aware of her coating of flour dust, her muddy feet, and the ring around her left ankle where the flour had met the mud and hardened into a gray paste.

"Have you given any thought to my proposal?" he asked as calmly as if he were asking for a bag of flour and not for the rest of her life.

"Errr," she said.

Young women married much older wealthy men all the time. It happened a lot. Childbearing was a dangerous business, and there were a lot of widowers out there. There was nothing unusual about it.

So why did this feel so wrong?

"You have a choice," said Crevan.

She should tell him no. If she told him no, he'd go away. They could all acknowledge that his offer had been a mistake. Aunt would never forgive her, but Aunt never forgave anything. She still hadn't forgiven Rhea for giving a beggar a loaf of bread five years ago and brought it up on special occasions.

Rhea opened her mouth, just as her father came around the side of the building.

"Milord," he said. "Milord, I saw your horse—forgive me, can we offer you any refreshment? Wine or ale?"

"No, indeed," said Lord Crevan, nodding to the miller. "I was just making the acquaintance of your daughter, in fact."

"Ah—errr—yes," said her father. "This is Rhea, then."

Rhea was slightly gratified to see that she wasn't the only one who was reduced to babbling by the lord, but she still wished he would do better. He was her father, after all, and the miller, one of the most respected men in town.

"Well?" asked Lord Crevan, a smile playing around his lips.

It took Rhea a moment to remember what he had asked, and then her heart, already sinking, seemed to settle in her toes.

"I—uh—I'm not sure."

The smile deepened. Rhea shot her father a pleading look.

"She's very flattered by your offer, milord," said her father firmly. "Is she?"

Rhea felt like a mouse caught in the mill gears. No matter what she did, they were going to grind her to bits. "Yes, very flattered," she said faintly.

"I am certain she will be worth it," Crevan said, and held out a hand.

Automatically, she held hers out to shake. He caught it instead, with a quick gesture that reminded her of the swan lunging for her lunch, and slid something cold onto her finger. Then he looked down at the silver ring—*an engagement ring, it's an engagement ring*—and smiled.

Before she could react, he brought her hand to his lips and kissed the back of it.

Rhea watched this with the expression of someone who had just been handed a dead flounder.

She had read about hand kissing. She knew it happened. It had always struck her as sort of romantic, and yes, she'd had a few day-dreams about meeting a man who would kiss her hand, and it would be like a lightning bolt through both of them, and then he'd tell her that he was really a prince wandering the land in search of the maiden of his heart, and, now that he'd found her, he would sweep her off her feet and take her back to his castle, and *she would never have to help dig an outhouse again.*

Rhea's imagination tended to get a little fuzzy after the bit where they got back to the castle, but the bit about the outhouses was very clear.

But this . . . this was nothing like those daydreams.

It wasn't that he slobbered or anything, but it was rather desperately embarrassing. It was *wrong*. Lords did not ride up on giant roan horses and kiss the hands of millers' daughters. Well, sometimes they did, but only ravishingly beautiful millers' daughters, like the ones in the stories, who were brave and true and fair. Rhea figured she was one for three on that list, since she mostly didn't lie unless it was really important. Probably no one truly brave would be terrified of swans.

She wanted to pull her hand away, but she didn't. Even if lords didn't do things like this, millers' daughters *definitely* didn't snub lords.

It didn't feel romantic. It felt like that moment in a conversation when someone has just said the wrong thing and everyone is standing around trying to figure out how to gloss it over and get past it. She felt embarrassed for everyone involved—for the lord, for herself, and for her father, who was, after all, watching the whole scene.

And then a spark jumped from his fingers to hers, or something that felt like a spark. She twitched and stared stupidly down at her hand. When she looked up again, Crevan was smiling.

It was a smug smile. Rhea didn't like it at all.

"I'll send for you," said Lord Crevan. And with that, he released her hand and turned away to his horse.

Miller and miller's daughter stood and watched him ride away. The horse looked ridiculously pink in the afternoon light, and it kicked up puffs of dust from the road.

"A fine gentleman," said her father, nodding to her. "You see?"

His voice was full of entreaty. He did not sound like one of the most important men in the village. He sounded hopeful and afraid.

Rhea looked down at her hand. It looked perfectly normal, but there was still a nasty tingling at the fingertips. She felt as if her hand had fallen asleep.

The sensation faded almost as soon as she noticed it, but it lingered longest around the silver ring.

She shook her hand once or twice, and then it was perfectly normal again.

"Huh," she said, and could think of nothing more to say.

The next morning, Rhea got up early and went into the village.

In the center of the village, at the crossing of the only two streets, stood the inn. It had no name, because it was the only inn in town, the same way that the mill was the only mill and Viscount Skeller was the only viscount. Rhea's friend Susannah worked there, by virtue of the fact that her mother owned it.

It was cool and dim inside, and the air danced with dust motes. Susannah was sweeping the floor and humming to herself.

"Rhea," she said. "What are you doing here?"

"I'm getting married," said Rhea grimly.

Susannah paused. "What, right this minute?"

"No," said Rhea, exasperated. "Not now, and not here. To a lord."

Her friend's eyes grew very round, and not entirely with delight. She dropped the broom. *"What?"*

"A lord," said Rhea. "I know. It doesn't make any sense to me, either. He's named Crevan. Do you know him?"

"Oh, him," said Susannah.

Rhea had a brief urge to scream. "You know him, too? Am I the only one in town who doesn't?"

Susannah sighed and picked the broom up again. She was short and plump and good-natured, and people assumed that she was a bit dim, which was a very foolish thing to assume.

"I don't know him," she said. "Not personally. But people talk about him sometimes. He's one of the viscount's friends from the capital. Doesn't live around here, but he comes out for the hunting. Some of the viscount's servants drink here during the season. They say he's a bit odd."

"Odd?" Rhea remembered the spark across her fingers. "Odd how?"

Susannah shrugged. "Well, he doesn't have a manservant. That's odd, if you're a lord."

Rhea sighed. She couldn't judge Crevan for not wanting someone to help him put his trousers on in the morning.

"Do they say why he might want to get married?"

"He's a widower, I think," said Susannah. "Isn't he? I think someone said that . . ."

"I wouldn't know." Rhea flung her hands in the air. "I don't know anything. I'd never seen him before yesterday, but apparently he's been watching me, and he made an offer for me, and I don't know why."

Susannah frowned. "That *is* odd," she said. "Um. I mean, it's very flattering, of course . . ."

"That's what my father says," said Rhea glumly.

"So you've met him now?" asked Susannah.

"Only briefly."

Her friend made a prodding gesture. "And . . . ?"

Rhea found that she had no idea what to say. *He's got a pink horse. He kissed my hand, and it was sort of awful. He makes my father babble, and I hate that. I don't trust him. There was a spark when he touched me.*

"He definitely is . . . a bit odd," she said finally, and grimaced. "Do you know anything else about him? Anything at all?"

"He rides by sometimes with the viscount," said Susannah. "There's not a lot of gossip about him, though. Not like Lord Glorian—his grooms come in, and they get roaring drunk and tell everybody all about how His Lordship's carrying on with the viscount's cousin."

"Good for the viscount's cousin," said Rhea, slumping against the bar. The polished wood counter dug into her back. "That doesn't help me very much, does it?"

"Well, it's not like they say he beats his horses or something," said Susannah. "And they would. That's something, isn't it?"

Rhea looked at her friend's worried pink face. She was trying to be reassuring. Rhea knew this and was touched by it, even if she didn't feel at all reassured.

She stared at the silver ring. The silence stretched out between them, almost visible, like the dust motes in the sunlight.

Susannah began sweeping again, although without much enthusiasm.

"I wanted to say no," said Rhea.

Her friend nodded slowly. "Your parents won't let you," she said. It wasn't a question, but Rhea answered it anyway.

"They think it's a great opportunity."

"Ha!" Susannah's laugh held very little humor. "Sure. They think that you don't turn down lords. They're right. There's a lot of gossip about what happens if you try." She attacked a stain on the floor, beating the broom's bristles against it.

"Gossip?" asked Rhea faintly.

Susannah's knuckles were white on the broom. "You know. If one of the viscount's sons decides to take up with a maid or something. They don't often ask what the maid wants, do they?"

Rhea stared at the stain. A servant girl from up at the manor house had drowned herself in the millpond years before. Rhea hadn't been allowed to see the body. She'd heard her aunt say that the girl had been no better than she should be, but nobody would tell her anything more about it. ("No better than she should be" was one of Aunt's strongest reproaches. Rhea had only heard her use it one other time, about a girl who had been heavily pregnant at her own wedding.)

Had the drowned girl turned down a lord? Or had she failed to turn one down and paid the price?

"I just wish I knew why he picked me," Rhea said.

Susannah sighed. "He was probably riding by the mill one day and saw you. You know you can't hear a thing with all the grinding. He could ride up to the doorstep before you heard him."

Rhea rubbed her thumb against the ring, frowning. This was entirely plausible, but why would the mere sight of her drive him to watch her from a distance and offer for her?

It doesn't make sense. None of this makes sense.

"You'll have to promise to come back when you're a grand lady," said Susannah, tucking her arm through Rhea's. "My mother will get you the very best wine in the house, and we'll drink to your health."

"Sure," said Rhea, unconvinced. Were great ladies allowed to go and drink in common inns? Would she even be allowed to see Susannah again?

She hugged her friend, and Susannah hugged back, and neither of them met the other's eyes.

Chapter Four

The basics of milling went like this: there was a waterwheel, and as the stream flowed by the mill, the current turned the waterwheel, which turned another wheel on a shaft, which turned a few other things hooked together, which ultimately turned a millstone. The millstone was very large and very heavy, and if you dumped grain under the stone beneath it, it would grind that grain into flour.

The millstone was quite indiscriminate, though, and it would also grind your fingers, toes, and other available bits of anatomy into flour. In order to cut down on the loss of extremities among millworkers, the grain was dumped into a hopper, which fed to the grinder through a sloped trough.

Rhea's father ran the mill, so he watched the various complicated turning bits to make sure nothing broke. He oiled things and occasionally replaced other things. He collected the milled flour into sacks, and twice a week he loaded the sacks into his wagon and distributed the flour to the farmers who owned the grain.

Rhea's aunt, who had the eyes of an eagle and the heart of a miser, supervised the weighing out of the grain.

Rhea's mother, who had a fine, neat hand, noted down the weights of each sack of grain, and who owned it, and who had paid for milling and who hadn't.

Rhea's job, which was utterly boring, was to thump the trough every few minutes to make sure the grain was sliding down at the proper rate and to make sure the hoppers didn't jam.

Where you got a lot of grain, you got a lot of mice, and where you got a lot of mice, sooner or later you got dead mice. It wasn't as bad as it could be, but every now and then, a dead mouse would fall into one of the hoppers and somebody with small hands had to reach way down in there and pull it out, or the whole system would back up. This was not a pleasant job, but at least it wasn't a regular one. No more than a few times a week.

Anyway, you cooked bread before you ate it, so if there were some little mousey fragments ground into the flour, it wasn't like it would hurt anything.

A couple of times a year, a gremlin would get into the mill. The mechanisms, with their big grinding gears and turning wheels and rotating shafts, were irresistible to gremlins. They thrived on sabotaging mechanical things; the more complicated the better.

They looked more or less like big mice wearing little tool belts, and it wasn't until you actually caught one stuck in the hopper and hauled it out that you saw the mouth full of small pointed teeth and the stubby little hand on the end of the tail.

Unlike mice, gremlins really were a problem. If you ground one into flour on accident, the bread had a tendency to explode in the oven, or bleed when you cut into it, or turn into a flock of starlings that would tear around the cottage, shrieking, and then people came around and had words with the miller, and many of the words had only four letters and involved hand gestures.

So as soon as you caught a gremlin, or heard a group of them giggling in the rafters, you had to run quick to the conjure wife, who lived outside the village in a hut that looked like it had been assembled from the less desirable bits of a goat.

The conjure wife kept a flock of bone-white quail, and after you told her your problem, she would send you out to the yard to catch one. Then she'd wring its neck, clean it, tie the bones and the feathers up in a little bag with a few herbs, and send you home with it. It looked the same every time, a grisly little package topped with a quail skull, no matter what the problem was—fever or gremlins or fits, cows not giving milk or goats getting the staggers, or potatoes hauling themselves out of the ground and sulking in the corner of the field. (Potatoes were, for some reason, more prone to fits of random magic than most vegetables. It would take a remarkable magic to affect turnips or kale. No one bothered planting eggplants—they would run into the woods or fly away on leafy kites the instant your back was turned.) But the conjure wife's quail charms worked, every time. You hung the sad little package in the doorway, and pretty soon, the gremlins were gone.

Gremlin infestations were a rare excitement. Most of Rhea's time was spent thumping the grain trough and checking the hopper for mice. This kept her hands busy while leaving her mind entirely free. She always spent a lot of time thinking, and this week had been no exception. She had a lot to think about, and even if the world had been turned upside down, the flour still had to get milled.

It did not seem fair. She was unwillingly engaged to a strange man. A strange man who had kissed her hand and ridden away on a big pink horse. That this could take place in a world that still, stubbornly, included flour sacks and grain and millstones and dead mice seemed like a poor job of management. She could understand why people didn't have much truck with gods anymore.

But the saints weren't of much help, either. She tried praying to the Lady of Stones—going so far as to stretch down and trail her fingers along the millstone as she did it, since it was common knowledge that if you held a stone while you prayed to her, it made the prayers work better—and then waited all day for word to come that Lord Crevan had fallen off his horse and broken his neck. It didn't happen. In fact, she saw him riding that evening, far off across the hillside, on the unmistakable roan horse.

So much for prayer, then. What was the point if the saints wouldn't kick someone off a horse when you asked them nicely?

"Feh," Rhea muttered, and thumped a fist into the trough, making the kernels rattle. "Stupid lord. Stupid saints. Stupid pink horse."

Suppose he is a magician.

The thought had hardly left her since his visit.

That odd tingle in her hand hadn't felt like static, and the way he had smiled—no, she would have laid money he was responsible for it.

Well, and what if he was? There was nothing inherently *wrong* with being magicky. Every village had its conjure wife to make the little charms and handle any stray bits of magic that made mischief. Barrelridge, forty miles away, even had a clockmaker who was a rat speaker. Rumor had it his clocks were the best because he equipped his familiars with tiny tools, and they made smaller gears and mechanisms than any human hand could.

And lots of people could do little things, whether from inheriting a few drops of magician's blood or from getting in the way of a bit of loose magic. Susannah could tell if beer had soured while it was still in the keg. One of Rhea's cousins could call frogs, which wasn't much good unless you had far too many insects in the garden, although she'd been a terror as a small child.

One of her other cousins had an extra toe, but there was probably nothing magical about that.

In the old days, there had been a lot more magic around—or so people said—but these days, it was all spread out. You got conjure wives and rat speakers, but not so many powerful magicians.

Not that you heard about anyway.

It wasn't that anyone looked down on magicians, but, well, you wanted to know where they were. People got antsy when you had a power they didn't have. Still, while it was understandable why a person wouldn't want others to know they were magicky, people who hid it were . . . *suspicious.*

And if Lord Crevan was a magician, he really should have said something before asking her to marry him. That was a lot more significant than having an extra toe.

Maybe that was his way of saying something. Maybe he was letting you know—you, and not your father.

This thought alarmed her enough that she missed her next swipe at the trough and banged her knuckles on the hopper instead. The silver ring went clink! as it struck.

"Ow!"

She rubbed her sore knuckles and thumped the trough with her shoulder instead.

Well. Suppose he *was* a magician?

Rhea stuck a knuckle in her mouth and considered.

It seemed like it should matter. It seemed like it should matter a *lot.*

More grain thumped down into the hopper.

Reluctantly, she decided that it didn't.

If she went to her parents and said, "Hey, I think Lord Crevan is a magician," they would probably just look at her and say, "Well, isn't that nice?" and absolutely nothing would change.

"I bet he's not a nice magician," she said aloud while the mill machinery ground on around her. Then, "I hope he's not like the conjure wife." The conjure wife was nice enough, but she was more than a little mad, and while you were glad to have her around the village, you certainly wouldn't want to marry her.

"The term is *sorcerer,*" said Lord Crevan from the doorway, raising his voice to be heard over the machinery. "And I am nothing like the conjure wife."

Rhea yelped, flung herself backward, and very nearly fell off the ladder. She got one arm hooked through it, and that brought her up short while her feet slithered down the rungs. Fortunately the ladder was bolted down, like everything else in the mill, or she would have fallen off and probably broken her neck.

"I—uh—Lord Crevan—"

She tried to curtsey, which is nearly impossible on a ladder, much less in breeches.

"Perhaps you could come down," said Lord Crevan, smiling faintly. Rhea was starting to dislike that smile a lot. It was the smile of a man who found nothing funny and everything amusing.

"Um." Rhea had a mad urge to climb back up to the hopper platform, but what good would that do?

Her father was out delivering sacks of flour, and her mother and aunt were weeding the garden. If they hadn't seen him come in, they probably weren't going to show up to help her, assuming that she needed help . . . and assuming that they could do anything about it.

We're engaged. This is . . . um . . . perfectly normal. We're getting to know each other before the wedding. That's all.

She found that she didn't believe that thought, even as she was thinking it.

Still, she couldn't very well stay on top of the ladder.

"What's the difference between a sorcerer and a magician?" she asked, climbing down. She concentrated on the rungs in front of her so she would not have to look at the tall man in the doorway.

"A sorcerer is one who practices magic with deliberation," he said. "Not one who possesses only the minor little talents that abound."

"Oh." The ladder was very short. Rhea was at the bottom much faster than she wanted to be. She wondered what "with deliberation" meant. "Errr. That's nice?"

Crevan smiled again.

So he's a sorcerer. I am marrying a sorcerer. No, that didn't seem right. She tried again—*A lord, who is also a sorcerer, is marrying a miller's daughter.*

That was easier. If she put it like that, it could be any miller's daughter, not her.

She'd read the word *sorcerer*, of course. But the books had never mentioned how they differed from any other magic folk. *With deliberation* wasn't a particularly helpful explanation.

Well. So can he turn me into a toad or something?

Was marrying him better or worse than being turned into a toad? She wasn't entirely certain.

Rhea shuffled out from behind the ladder, feeling small and dusty and grubby. Crevan was wearing white again. His clothes shone like a swan's feathers.

She made it as far as one of the wooden pillars, fetched up against it, and couldn't make herself go any farther. Through the open doorway, she could see the back end of Crevan's big pink horse.

You'd think if he were that good of a magician, he'd be able to turn his horse some color other than pink . . .

"Come to my house," he said abruptly. "Three days from now."

"What?"

"Are you hard of hearing? I can speak more loudly if you are."

Rhea flushed. She felt blood rushing into her face—her cheeks tingly, then hot. Her head ached.

There were so many things she wanted to say, but she could not think of any of them. Except *no*, and that didn't seem like a wise thing to say.

"You don't turn down lords," Susannah had said. "There's a lot of gossip about what happens if you try."

You didn't hear as much gossip in a mill as you did in an inn. Rhea was starting to regret that lack.

"I didn't know you had a house near here, milord."

"There are many things you do not know, little Rhea."

She put her hands behind her so he could not see that they were clenched into fists. *You don't turn down lords.*

"How will I find your house?" she asked at last.

"North, from the spring, into the wildwood. There's a road. Set out at dusk," he said. "The road is very white in the moonlight. You will not go astray."

"*North* of the spring?" Rhea had been to that spring a hundred times and knew perfectly well that there was no road there.

"There is a road," he said again.

"At *night?*" said Rhea, who didn't quite dare to argue. Still—*We aren't married yet! You don't spend the night at a man's house, even if you're planning on marrying him. People would think . . . Well, who knows what people would think?*

"Are you afraid?" he asked. His smile was lazy and cruel, and she didn't like it at all.

"No—yes! The woods are full of wild animals, and bandits, and—and—who knows what—"

"Not these woods," he said. "Not along the white road. Though I would not recommend leaving it."

"But—"

"Until then," he said. He moved closer, and Rhea wanted to back up, but she couldn't. You didn't back away from your fiancé, and anyway, the ladder would have blocked her path.

He bowed and kissed her hand again.

The pink horse's hooves clattered merrily along the road as he rode away. Rhea wiped her hand against her breeches. His lips hadn't been particularly damp, but there seemed to be a weight where they had touched, as if her skin were heavier.

Chapter Five

"Set out at night?" said her aunt. "Well, that's unusual, but doubtless there's a good reason."

They were in the cottage, and Rhea was having a bath in the copper tub before the fire. She was not enjoying it, but she had not enjoyed anything since Lord Crevan had come three days ago and told her where to find his house.

"Good reason? What possible reason could there *be*?"

Her mother sat in the corner, spinning, not looking at Rhea. Her face was very still, but her hands were restless.

Rhea spluttered as her aunt dumped a ewer of water over her head. "Perhaps he'll be away until late that day, on business."

"Then—Pfffbt! Spleh!—why not have me come another day?"

Her aunt frowned down at her. "I'm sure he has a reason right enough. Keep civil, Rhea, and don't borrow trouble. This is a great opportunity for you, if you mind your manners and don't drive him away with your tongue."

"But—"

"No buts!"

"But how come nobody knows he's got a house near town? I asked Susannah. She said he lives in the capital."

"Susannah doesn't know everything," said her aunt. "And perhaps he just keeps to himself and minds his own business. Which Susannah ought to consider doing."

She dumped another ewer of water, and Rhea's attempt to defend her friend was lost to spluttering.

"It might be a hunting lodge that he closes up for the season," said her aunt while Rhea tried to shake water out of her ears. "The viscount probably leases him the land. Could use a woman's touch, I'm sure."

"But you don't go to strange men's houses if you aren't married!"

There was a clatter. Her mother had dropped the spindle.

Her aunt scowled fiercely, which was what she did when she couldn't think of anything to say.

"I'm sure it'll be fine," said Rhea's mother.

Rhea recognized her tone of voice. She'd heard it before, last spring, when her mother had convinced her father to wait out a really fantastic storm in the cottage instead of running to check on the mill. "I'm sure it'll be fine," she'd said, not because she expected it to be fine, but because it didn't matter whether it was fine or not—there wasn't anything to be done, and there was no sense in being miserable about it.

She could see, in an odd way, what they were doing.

It was as if the words they spoke were weaving a kind of net, a net of normalcy and propriety and sanity, around a situation that was anything but.

The proposition that Lord Crevan had made was *not* normal. Betrothed girls did not go alone to the houses of relative strangers, even the strangers to whom they were betrothed. Certainly not when no one else even knew he had a house, and she only knew that it lay tucked in the dark forest.

They *definitely* didn't set out into the woods at night looking for such a house.

The whole thing was just this side of indecent.

But they were creating their net with comments like "Well, certainly he'll feed you when you get there, I shouldn't say" and "Think how lovely it will be to see the house you'll be the lady of," as if they could catch the indecency in it like a fish.

As if, by pretending everything was perfectly normal, it would *make* things perfectly normal.

"It won't work," she said to herself later, having a good sulk down at the unplowed end of the field. "Pretending it's normal won't actually *change* anything."

They know that, said the voice in the back of her head, which usually sounded tired, and a bit exasperated. *But what else can they do?*

"They don't have to make me go! They didn't have to make me get engaged! Lord Crevan *said* I had a choice!"

Do you really think he meant that? asked the voice at the back of her head in a tone of mild inquiry.

She inhaled.

Because of course, it wasn't *really* a choice, was it? It was like when the viscount's rent collector came around twice a year and said, "Have you got twenty silver dirhams then?" It wasn't really a question. It meant "You'd better have the money" or a really good explanation, like a live badger currently sitting on the strongbox.

You couldn't *not* pay the rent. Her family had been millers since time out of mind, the mill itself had been constructed more generations ago than anybody knew, but they didn't own the mill. The lord did. That was just the way it worked.

And while Viscount Skeller was a pretty good lord, everyone said, who had been understanding about the current lean times, who held a fine feast for everyone twice a year, and who didn't uphold any indecent customs like riding off with young peasant lasses on their wedding night or hunting two-legged deer, he was still the lord.

Rhea wondered briefly if it would do any good to appeal to the viscount for help. Could she go to him and say that a lord was forcing her to marry him?

Ah.

Her lips twisted as she found the answer, like a terrier finding a rat. There it was. Lord Crevan had *asked* for her, not ordered. If she or her father went to the viscount, Crevan could say, with perfect honesty, that he'd given her a choice, he'd asked her father for her hand without compelling her in any way, and he wouldn't be lying, even if it wasn't quite true.

It would all look perfectly decent if the viscount asked. And at the end of day, it wouldn't matter, because while you didn't turn down lords, you especially didn't turn down lords who were also magicians.

You don't know that. He said he was a sorcerer, but he hasn't done any-thing . . . anything magicky. Well, other than the spark, and it might have been static. Besides, being a magician doesn't make you bad.

He's just a little . . . off *somehow.*

It could be anything.

Well, it seemed that she would find out.

Freshly scrubbed, her eyes still smarting from soap, Rhea slunk out of the cottage and toward the opposite end of the village.

She was familiar with the path, which took less than ten minutes at a brisk walk, but it wasn't one she went down often. Not since the last time they'd had gremlins.

The conjure wife's yard was small and dusty. Her hut had weeds growing out of the thatch, and had for as long as Rhea could remember. Some of those weeds were quite large by now—well on their way to being respectably sized trees.

White quail roamed the yard, scratching at the dust. A few were picking at seedlings in one corner, and one had gotten up onto the roof.

The ones on the ground scattered as she approached. They had dark eyes and pale-gray topknots that bobbed as they ran.

Rhea steeled herself to knock on the door, but it banged open before she got within five feet of it.

"Eh?" said the conjure wife, blinking at her from the shadows. "Eh? Miller, aren't you? Gremlins again?"

"No gremlins," said Rhea. "Um. I'm getting married."

The conjure wife raised an eyebrow. She was not terribly old, but her hair was as white as the quail and straggled out from her skull like ragged flower petals. "Yes? Want a potion to put fire back into an old man, or take it out again? Eh?"

"No!" said Rhea, a bit shocked at the idea. *I'm too young—he's not—it's not like that.*

It had better not *be like that!*

"His name's Lord Crevan," she blurted. "He says he's a sorcerer."

The conjure wife sucked air through her teeth. She was missing one of the front ones, but you rarely noticed, because she didn't often smile. "Men say a lot of things," she said.

"But could he be a sorcerer? What's a sorcerer anyway?"

"Magic like paper," said the conjure wife. "Everything written down and tied up in words. Don't know him. Don't deal with lords. Lords go to sorcerers. Only a conjure wife, me."

Rhea sighed. She'd hoped that the conjure wife could tell her something—anything—that might be useful. Even knowing if Crevan really was a sorcerer would have been helpful. At least then she wouldn't wonder.

The conjure wife sniffed the air like a dog. "Got a smell on you, girl," she said.

"I just took a bath."

"Not like that." She stepped out of the hut, still sniffing. "Smells like magic. Maybe sorcery. Don't know."

The woman circled around Rhea once and then grabbed her wrist. "There," she said, pointing. "That."

Rhea followed the line of her finger to the silver engagement ring.

A heavy feeling turned in her stomach and settled somewhere below her heart.

"He gave it to me," she said. "Can you . . . um . . . de-magic it?"

"Ha! Me? No."

Rhea thought of taking the ring off, but then he'd ask where it was, and she'd have to put it on again. And if it was magic, would he know somehow that she had taken it off?

He was watching me before, he said. For all I know, he's watching me now.

She looked around, suddenly suspicious, but the trees leaned closely around the conjure wife's yard, and if a man on horseback was lurking in the woods, she could not see him.

"Sorcerer," said the conjure wife, peering at the ring. "Could be. Could be. Won't say he's not."

"I'm supposed to go to his house tonight."

The conjure wife smelled strong as a goat, and her eyes had white all around the irises. But she squeezed Rhea's wrist clumsily, and Rhea realized that she meant it as comfort.

"Can't see the future," she said. "Never could. Not my skill." One fingertip hovered over the ring, but she didn't touch it. "Going to dark places, though, if you follow this. Don't have to see the future to know that."

"I'll be careful," said Rhea, because she had to say something.

"No point being careful. Careful won't help." She released Rhea's arm and stepped away. The quail came running around her feet as if they were chicks, and she knelt down and spread her arms over them. They chirped and crouched as if they had seen the shadow of a hawk overhead.

"Be smart," said the conjure wife. "And lucky. Lucky's good, too."

Chapter Six

She set out at dusk.

Her aunt looked her over and gave a single huff of approval. She had wanted Rhea to wear the red dress that Crevan had given her, but Rhea had managed to convince her that the dress would be torn if she went traipsing through the woods in it. It was a small rebellion, but it seemed to be the only one that Rhea was going to get.

The red dress was in her pack. She was under orders to change into it as soon as humanly possible.

Her mother hugged her fiercely. "Be polite," she said. "Be courteous. Be safe." And then, her voice dropping to a whisper in Rhea's ear, "Be *careful*."

She turned away quickly. It occurred to Rhea that her mother was crying, which made her feel like crying herself.

They tried to weave that net, but they can't quite hide the fact that this is wrong, this is strange, this isn't normal . . .

"I'll come with you as far as the spring," said her father, picking up his walking stick.

"Um," said Rhea. "Okay. Thank you."

She looked back at the cottage, feeling like she should say or do something—but there was nothing to be done, and everything had been said already. She picked up one foot and put it in front of the other, and then did it again, and then her father was walking beside her, and she heard the door of the cottage close behind them.

They walked in silence. The spring was only about half a mile away, not far, but the path seemed longer in the dark. Crickets chirped and buzzed in the hedgerows, and bullfrogs croaked pitilessly in the shadows.

"I don't like this," said Rhea when it seemed like the silence was filling up her throat, and she had to say something or strangle on it.

"Nor do I," said her father.

Rhea sagged a little. He didn't like it. He knew it was wrong. And yet they were still walking together to the spring.

They reached the spring. It was not particularly impressive at this time of year—no more than a dull little seep over the stones. In damper seasons, it was covered in moss, but now the outer edges of moss had gone dry and baked in the heat.

On the north side of the spring was the wildwood.

"There is a road," Lord Crevan had said.

Rhea didn't see any sign of it.

Is this going to be magic? Oh, Lady of Stones, I bet it is . . .

She walked toward the wildwood, aware that her father was still standing beside the spring. What would she do if there wasn't a road? Could she go home? Maybe she could. If Lord Crevan showed up again, she could just say that she'd looked, and there wasn't a road, and it wasn't like she could crash through the wildwood at night and—

There wasn't a road.

There was a path.

It didn't look much bigger than a deer trail, the kind of track worn by animals coming to the spring to drink. A road was something you drove carts and oxen down. You could ride a horse down a road. Lord

Crevan couldn't possibly ride his stupid pink horse down this little twisty track, but he expected *her* to follow it, a fact that struck Rhea as enormously unfair.

Her father came up beside her and looked down the deer trail. "Is that it?" he asked.

"I guess," said Rhea. "He said north of the spring."

"Well," said her father doubtfully, "I suppose he could have a hunting lodge in the woods there . . ." (Which was ridiculous, Rhea thought, because if a lord's hunting lodge had been that close to the village, everybody would know about it, but she didn't say it out loud, because everything was awful enough already.)

He hugged her. "Be careful," he whispered, as if he didn't dare say it aloud. And then, miserably, "I'm sorry."

Rhea hated Crevan in that moment, not for forcing her to marry him, which was bad enough, but for doing this to her father. Her father was a good man. He was a good miller, and he kept Aunt from cheating the farmers, and he donated money to the church, and when the barn cat had kittens, he never drowned any of them. He didn't deserve for some noble to put him in this position.

But here they were. And they both knew that if she went, it might be bad, but if she didn't go, it would *definitely* be bad. For all of them.

Rhea took a deep breath.

"I should go," she said, and her father nodded. She stepped onto the deer trail, putting up an arm to fend off the branches that reached for her eyes.

She wanted to look back at him, but it was immediately dark and she had to feel her way forward in the blackness, moving one careful step at a time. The roots were humped and tangled and seemed to heave under her feet, and the branches clawed at her.

Something ran across the back of her hand, and she shrieked and shook her arm, and the branch she'd been holding back whipped around and smacked her across the forehead.

Now she was *really* mad.

Rhea snarled, stomping forward, not caring if she fell down and scraped her shins on the roots. She wanted out, out, *out!*

And then the trees opened up around her, and the white road spread before her, gleaming like bone in the moonlight.

Chapter Seven

The road was white, just as he'd described it. It was edged with a few feet of brittle grass, and then the grass turned into the dense tangle of the wildwood. The road itself was as clear as heartbreak.

Rhea turned around and saw that the road ran behind her as well, apparently to the clearing with the spring. Her father was nowhere to be seen.

Magic.

Well then.

"There is a road," Lord Crevan had said.

And such a road. The cobbles were white and round as skulls. Red leaves washed like blood beneath the trees, making dark puddles under the moon.

She took a step forward. She didn't want to, but the alternative was to stand there until daybreak, because she already knew that she couldn't go back.

She took another step.

The sound of the crickets was muffled now, but there were other noises from the wildwood—bugs, birds, tree limbs. She could hear a whip-poor-will off in the distance, shouting whip-poor-*will*!

whip-poor-*will*! in defiance of any others of his kind that might be nearby.

She kept walking.

Her anger drained out of her with every step, like water sloshing out of a bucket. What did it matter if she was angry? The white road didn't care. Lord Crevan didn't care. Her anger made no difference at all.

Nothing Rhea did made any difference at all.

Something groaned in the woods that definitely wasn't a whip-poor-will. It was a gassy bubbling noise, like a belch.

Did bears belch? What about trolls?

She kept walking, her footsteps slow and plodding. The road shone savagely before her, and she might as well have been a dark-shelled beetle crawling along it. There was a bear or a troll or maybe a giant, savage, man-eating whip-poor-will in the woods.

She didn't realize she was crying until the road had become too blurred to see, and then a great aching sob came up her throat, and she staggered sideways off the road and into the grass.

It's all very well to cry for any number of reasons, including the fact that sometimes you simply need a good cry. And since a lot of the reasons for crying occur largely in your head—which is not to say that they're not real—it usually helps. Perhaps the world won't have changed for the better after five or ten minutes spent sobbing into a pillow, but at least you won't feel quite so much like crying. The red hollow under your breastbone is emptied out, and things can be faced with more resolution. (And a swollen nose and itchy eyes, of course, but you can't have everything.)

The problem with crying in the woods, by the side of a white road that leads somewhere terrible, is that the reason for crying *isn't* inside your head. You have a perfectly legitimate and pressing reason for crying, and it will still be there in five minutes, except that your throat will be raw and your eyes will itch and absolutely nothing else will have changed.

Rhea's throat was raw and her eyes itched, and she realized that she didn't have a handkerchief. Her face was wet with tears and all the other unfortunate fluids that distinguish a really good cry, and the lack of a handkerchief seemed like a whole new reason to cry.

She hunched down and put her forehead on her knees and made a low, animal sound of misery.

She was feeling so wretched that it took several minutes for her to realize something was touching her leg.

Rhea looked up.

There was a hedgehog sitting next to her, with one small paw pressed against her thigh.

She made the awkward gulping noise of someone who is trying to stop crying because something completely unexpected has just occurred.

The hedgehog saw that it had her attention and held up something in its paw.

It was a leaf.

She stared at the leaf. It was rather large and silvery, with a slight fuzziness to it.

The hedgehog bobbed its head and pushed the leaf toward her in an unmistakable gesture.

The smaller part of her brain had stopped crying and was saying *No. No, no, no. This is crazy. This is not normal hedgehog behavior.*

However, the larger part of her brain, the automatic part that covered her mouth when she sneezed and said "Excuse me" when she moved through a crowd, felt that all such concerns were secondary, because she needed a handkerchief *right now*. Things were happening in her nose that needed to be stopped immediately.

She took the leaf and wiped her face and blew her nose. It was a very soft, very absorbent leaf. The hedgehog obviously knew what it was doing.

"Thank you," she said hoarsely.

The hedgehog nodded.

This is not normal.

It was quite an ordinary-looking hedgehog. It was six or seven inches long, and prickly. Its face was small and pointed, with large dark eyes.

"Are you really a hedgehog?" she asked, gulping a bit. "Are you a fairy or a person under a spell or something?"

The hedgehog shook its head.

"No, you're not a fairy, or no, you're not a hedgehog?"

The anatomy of hedgehogs makes it nearly impossible for one to put its paws on its hips, but it managed a fair approximation.

Rhea tried again. "Are you really a hedgehog?"

It nodded.

"Um." The little voice in her head, yelling about normal hedgehog behavior, was starting to get very loud. "You seem very smart for a hedgehog?"

It shrugged.

"I don't suppose—and I realize this is completely insane—but you don't *talk*, do you?"

For having such a small face, the hedgehog could manage quite a scathing look of disgust. Rhea found that she was rather relieved. Children's stories aside, there would have been something quite horrible about a talking hedgehog.

She sighed and rubbed a hand over her face. "I'm sorry. I'm . . . I have to go along the road. To the hunting lodge, you know."

The hedgehog frowned. It waved its front paws across each other and shook its head in a clear warning.

"I know," Rhea said. "I don't want to go. I just don't have any choice." She could feel another sob lurking in her chest, and squelched it. It's one thing to cry by yourself, and quite another to cry in front of a stranger, even if the stranger is only a hedgehog.

The hedgehog dropped to all fours and trundled up to the white road, where it stopped. The moonlight caught in its prickles as it gazed up the length of the road, seemingly deep in thought.

After a moment, it turned and came back. It sat up again and held up its paws, like a child asking to be picked up.

"You want me to carry you?"

It nodded.

"Errr—you want to come with me? To the lodge?"

It nodded again.

"Oh. Um. Are you sure?"

It was starting to get impatient. A hedgehog hopping irritably on its hind legs is a tragic sight. Rhea reached down and lifted the animal cautiously in both hands.

The prickles were indeed prickly, but not sharp enough to break the skin. The hedgehog wriggled a bit, settled its spines like a woman arranging her skirts, and nodded to her.

"Are we ready to go then? Um. Okay."

She stepped back onto the white road.

It was still white, and it still glowed under the moon, and the cobbles were still as rounded as old skulls, and the leaves still looked like splashes of blood across the stones, but Rhea felt better. She was still going somewhere terrible, but she had a hedgehog, dammit.

It wasn't that having a hedgehog was necessarily going to do her any good—she couldn't think of any stories where a wicked wizard had been brought low by a hedgehog, and anyway, she couldn't even swear that Crevan actually *was* a wicked wizard—but it is somehow easier to face things when one is not alone. Courage still does most of the heavy lifting, but Pride gets its shoulder in there, too, just to keep you from embarrassing yourself in front of the other person . . . or hedgehog, as the case may be.

Leaves crunched under her feet as she walked.

After about twenty minutes, her arms started to get tired.

"Do you suppose I could put you in a pocket?" she asked.

The hedgehog considered this, then nodded. Rhea opened the pocket in her skirt and slipped the hedgehog into it. There was a prickly shifting against her leg, and then the hedgehog got itself straightened out and poked its nose up over the top.

They kept walking.

The trees began to close in again. The drifting leaves grew thicker, throwing dark tendrils across the road and occasionally blowing and skittering in the wind. Though they moved like living things, the noise they made was dry and dead.

Rhea's jaw ached from clenching her teeth. The noises behind her scraped on her nerves. It was like walking through a crowd of mummified mice that stood up and danced as soon as your back was turned.

The trees were thick enough now that the white road was more of a deep-blue-and-black road, with occasional white spots, the color of an enormous mottled bruise.

They kept walking.

Then the trees stopped. Rhea saw the moonlight like a blue-white wall in front of her and stepped nervously out into it. To her eyes, which had gotten used to the dark under the trees, the open road blazed like noon.

There was a kind of cleared corridor around the road, with the trees pushed back a good fifty feet on either side. Grass grew along the verge. Weeds spread broad leaves over the ground or lifted seed heads into the air. It was not well tended, and yet the plants seemed to be avoiding the white stones.

Over the road was an arch of black wrought iron.

Sitting on top of the arch was a bird.

The hedgehog shifted in her pocket and made a mistrustful snorting noise.

Rhea reached down and brushed the prickles of its head with her fingers. "I don't like this either," she whispered.

It huffed a bit, but settled.

The bird looked like a crow, or rather, it looked more like a crow than it looked like anything else. Its beak was serrated like a bread knife, and parts of its skin gleamed in the moonlight in a way that wasn't quite normal for feathers.

When Rhea and her passenger were almost to the archway, the bird opened its eyes.

Rhea inhaled sharply. If not for the fact that the hedgehog was watching, it might have been a yelp.

The crow had two round stones for eyes, tied around the middle with cord. The sound of its eyelids sliding over the lumps of cord was a dry scrape, like the sound of the leaves blowing over the road.

It turned its head, sharp and birdlike, and she realized that the strange gleam was from bare skin. The top of its head was bald and leathery, the color of old jerky, and there was pale stitching that ran from the edges and vanished under its feathers. The feathers themselves were gray and dull and leaked ragged bits of down.

The whole bird looked dead, except for the fact it was moving.

Then it spread its wings, and she gasped.

The wings were crowlike enough, where they beat the air, but down its neck, running the length of the body, was a Y-shaped panel of bare flesh, held together with more rough cord.

It took her a moment to recognize the shape. Rhea had helped her mother gut chickens before, but the usual way was to go in through the bottom, so that you had a bird you could stuff later. But the other way to do it, if you didn't care how you were going to cook it afterward, was to cut it open from the neck on down.

The bird *had* been dead. And somebody had cut it open and put stone eyes in its head and sewn it back together and notched its beak and made it alive again.

She had a feeling she knew who had done it.

The bird golem's serrated beak creaked open, like pinking shears, and a voice came out. From her pocket, the hedgehog hissed.

"Be . . . bold . . . ,"

breathed the thing that wasn't quite a crow.

That's easy for it to say, said the voice inside her head sarcastically.

That was fine. As long as her attention was focused on the voice in her head, she didn't have to notice how badly her hands were shaking.

"Do you belong to Crevan?" she asked, and was quite surprised at how strong her voice sounded. There was hoarseness down in its depths, but it did not tremble.

The serrated beak creaked open.

"Be . . . bold . . . ,"

it said again.

"You said that already," she muttered. The bird golem cocked its head, and then, very slowly, the eyelids slid down over the stone eyes again.

She wondered if it could fly at all.

"Be bold, be bold . . . ," she said to herself. *What kind of advice is that? Is advice from an animate thing made of cords and stones and dead crow to be trusted anyway?*

The hedgehog shifted impatiently in her pocket. She squared her shoulders and walked through the arch.

The back of her neck prickled. She almost expected the bird golem to strike at her, but nothing happened.

When she was a dozen steps along, she turned and looked back at the iron arch. The golem was hunched and dark and looked like nothing alive, as if the maker of the arch had included some irregular bit of decoration that hadn't quite worked out.

They kept walking.

* * *

The wind died. It seemed that neither wind nor rain had troubled the road for some time along this stretch. White dust had filled up the spaces between the cobblestones. It puffed up with every step and hung drifting in the air. When Rhea glanced over her shoulder, her footsteps seemed to smoke behind her.

She could see something in the distance. The hedgehog, who had snuggled down into her pocket, shifted, and its pointed face peered over the pocket's edge once more.

It was another arch. There were two more dark lumps on it, huddled together at one end, as if for warmth.

Two sets of cord-wrapped stones opened and watched Rhea's approach. The hedgehog huffed its annoyance from her pocket.

The one on the left flapped its wings. It had the Y-shaped cut down its belly, but most of its head still had feathers on it. The serrated beak creaked open.

"Be bold . . . be bold . . ."

The second bird golem had only one leg. The other ended in a stump wrapped with wire. The wire glittered in the moonlight and made a thin metallic clink against the iron of the arch. Once its partner had spoken, it opened its beak and breathed,

". . . but not too bold . . ."

The hedgehog hissed.

Rhea found that in addition to being terrified and upset, she was now also rather annoyed. This was stupid. Be bold, but not too bold? Too bold about what? Where was she supposed to be bold?

Some specifics would be nice. Be bold for the next fifty steps, then not too bold for the next hundred, say.

"That's not very helpful," she told them.

The bird golems folded up their wings and lapsed back into silence.

She stalked under the arch and down the white road. When she kicked at the stones, the white dust roiled up nearly to her knees, and the hedgehog gave an indignant sneeze from her pocket.

"Sorry," she muttered. "But if you're going to go to all the trouble of setting up dead birds on the road to deliver messages, they should at least say something useful."

The annoyance was helpful. It pushed back the fear and made a clear space in her head where she could think. If she concentrated on the stupidity of reanimating a bird just so that it could deliver a message that didn't make very much sense, she wasn't thinking about what lay at the end of the white road.

She was so determinedly not thinking about the end of the road, in fact, that it came as a shock when she looked up and it was right in front of her.

The road swept up to a high black arch, and on the other side, it opened into a broad white courtyard. A fountain stood in the center, the water glittering so silver in the moonlight that it seemed like it should chime like coins when it tumbled back into the basin. The house on the other side was a huge crouching darkness under the trees.

That is not *a hunting lodge.*

It was a manor.

It was not possible that there was a manor house of this size—bigger even than the one belonging to the viscount—anywhere near the village. Everyone would know about it. You couldn't just hide a building this grand off in the woods somewhere.

And yet there it was.

Magic, thought Rhea. Was this what sorcery let you do—hide an enormous house in the middle of nowhere?

This was as far beyond rat speakers and conjure wives as Rhea could imagine.

On the black iron arch, there sat three birds. Two were clustered tightly together, their wings around each other. The third bird sat alone, on the other side of the arch, pointedly not looking at the other two.

Rhea felt her heart quail at the sight of the dark house, but she shoved it back. She stomped up to the arch and glared at the golems.

"Well?"

The two on the left looked down at her. The third bird did not.

> *"Be bold . . . be bold . . .*
> *But not too bold . . . ,"*

whispered the birds on the left, and then they bent their heads down against each other's stitched breasts as if in some terrible sorrow.

The third bird golem had almost no feathers left. Its body appeared hard and waxy in the moonlight. The wings looked like a net of wires with a few tattered tufts stuck in it.

It did not look at her. Its beak creaked open, and it said,

". . . or your heart's blood shall run cold."

"Well, that rhymed at least," Rhea snapped, "but it still isn't very useful advice."

The hedgehog shook a tiny paw at the bird and snorted angrily, which fed her courage. She put her hands on her hips. "Is that the best you've got?"

The bird golem's head snapped around suddenly, and it rocked forward. Rhea jerked back as the golem crawled over the arch, using its wire wings like claws. The hedgehog hissed, but the creature ignored it, hanging from the metal of the arch and thrusting its beak toward her face.

She was less than a foot from the bird golem. She could see a fine, hairy haze, made of old bits of down and dust and grit, covering the creature.

The beak opened. Its tongue was a small dry nub like a blackened nut.

". . . this . . . is a murderer's . . . house . . . ,"

whispered the dead bird.

Rhea stumbled backward. Her foot turned on one of the round stones, and she sat down hard. In her pocket, the hedgehog squeaked in alarm.

The thing to do at this point, she knew, the sane and sensible thing, would be to get up and turn around and run down the white road until she was home.

She didn't, for a couple of reasons.

The first one was that nothing had actually changed. Peasants still didn't disobey nobles, and if she came back to her family with a demented story about sewn-up dead birds with stone eyes talking . . . well, they might believe her, but then again, they might not. And she would have failed to turn up at the appointed time, and Lord Crevan did not seem like a particularly forgiving man.

The second reason was that the whole situation was just *wrong*.

It didn't make any sense.

Crevan had gone to all the trouble of setting up a half-dozen bird golems to guard the entrance to his house, and he'd even given them a bit of rhyming doggerel to memorize, presumably to warn off intruders. Certainly they would have been quite effective against traveling salesmen. But he'd invited her here—ordered her, if she were being honest—and it made no sense to invite her here, just to warn her off with his creepy dead birds.

Either he was mad—or stupid—or this was some kind of test.

Rhea was quite sure he wasn't stupid. He had handled her father much too efficiently for that.

He didn't strike her as mad, either. Young Brad, the wheelwright's son, had been fool enough to walk through a fairy ring one night, and when the fairies threw him back a week later (Rhea suspected they'd found him as boring as everyone else did), he was as mad as the mist and moonlight. He spent most of his time dancing very slowly in the middle of the road, and was generally harmless. Occasionally he'd take it in his head to put his trousers on the pig, much to the annoyance of both his mother and the pig.

Lord Crevan was not mad, as she understood it. He had probably never put trousers on a pig in his life.

That left the possibility that he was testing her.

Perhaps he was trying to see if she was brave.

"On the other hand," she said to the hedgehog, "this could be a test to see if I'm sensible, since the sensible thing to do would be to go home."

What was the worst that could happen if she turned and fled? Maybe he wouldn't marry her. That would be the very opposite of bad.

Assuming he doesn't say anything to the viscount about it. Assuming that the viscount doesn't decide that embarrassing his friend makes the millers more trouble than they're worth.

No, if this was a test, she was supposed to go forward, not back.

Still, none of it made any sense. If you were a murderer, would you really guard your home with birds saying, "Hi, I'm a murderer"? It lacked subtlety. But would anyone believe you?

No, they wouldn't. That's the beauty of it.

You probably *could* say, "I'm a murderer," and get just as many houseguests. People wouldn't believe you'd admit a thing like that. They'd think you were joking. Rhea didn't quite believe it herself.

She sighed and ran a hand through her hair. Up on the arch, the bird golem had resumed its post, stone eyes gazing into the distance.

"Do you think I should go on?" she asked the hedgehog, who had climbed out of her pocket to sit on her knee.

The hedgehog nodded, then shook its head, then lifted its front paws in the air and let them drop.

I don't know why I'm second-guessing Crevan's sanity—I'm sitting here talking to a hedgehog mime.

"You don't know? The answer's complicated?" she guessed.

It nodded.

"Should I go on to the house?"

It shifted from foot to foot and looked over its shoulder at the house. Then it nodded, although not with much enthusiasm.

"Is there some reason I shouldn't go back?" she tried.

The hedgehog nodded violently, and its quills rippled with a shudder.

"Something bad will happen if I go back." (More nodding.)

"But it won't happen if I keep going." (A shrug.)

"Will something bad happen if I go forward?" (Another shrug.)

Rhea rubbed her forehead. She was getting a serious headache. "Is whatever will happen if I go back worse than whatever will happen if I go forward?" (A definite nod.)

You do realize you're listening to a hedgehog, the voice in her head said. *Just thought I'd mention that.*

"How do you know this?" she asked.

It tapped its nose and spread its paws.

"Too complicated a question, sorry." This was worse than when the girls tried to tell the future by throwing pinecones in the fire and watching how they fizzled and popped. You couldn't get much more than yes or no out of the pinecones—and even that required some imagination—but the questions were at least frivolous ones like "Will I marry a rich man?," not "Am I about to be horribly murdered?"

"Am I about to be horribly murdered?"

The hedgehog shrugged, but then reached out and put a gentle paw on the back of her hand. It looked at her solemnly. Its eyes were dark and kind, and they held hers for a long moment.

Its sympathy was oddly steadying. Rhea squared her shoulders and nodded. "Okay. I can handle this." She paused. "Are you *sure* you're a hedgehog?"

It threw its paws in the air and huffed in evident disgust before returning to the safety of her pocket.

She stood up and took a step forward, then stopped as if she'd run into an iron bar. A thought had occurred to her, and not a pleasant one. She held the pocket open and looked down at the hedgehog.

"If I did go back—is there something on the road behind me?"

The hedgehog nodded.

"Something bad."

The hedgehog made a kind of grabbing, swooping gesture with both paws in front of its chest. Rhea couldn't quite make out what it was meant to show—there are limits to the expressiveness of hedgehog feet, particularly when the animal is on its back in somebody's pocket—but when the hedgehog then rolled into a tight ball, she got the gist well enough.

"Ah."

She let the pocket fall closed. The skin between her shoulder blades was crawling, but she did not look over her shoulder. Looking over her shoulder could not possibly help matters.

She walked forward, under the arch. Overhead, the two bird golems held each other tightly, and the third stared off into the forest and clicked its dead claws against the iron.

Click . . . click . . . click . . .

She entered the courtyard of Lord Crevan's house.

Chapter Eight

The fountain threw spray ten feet in the air. The patter of water on the basin was too much like the click of dried leaves on the white road for comfort.

The figure of a winged woman stood atop the fountain, wings extended. Rhea had seen statues of winged people before—the church-yard had several angels carved on top of tombstones—but unlike those of the angels, the wings of the figure on the fountain sagged exhaustedly.

Rhea gave the fountain a wide berth. She was cold and miserable and scared, and being wet wouldn't help in the least.

A broad cobblestone circle led around the fountain, probably suit-able for carriages, if one were ever to come up the white road. It seemed unlikely. There was moss growing between the stones, and plants grew in a thick tangle around the edges. Late flowers bloomed in what was clearly some kind of garden, although their cheerful colors were bleached by the moonlight.

"Those are black-eyed Susans," Rhea told the hedgehog. "And ploughman's wort and love-lies-bleeding and asters. I don't think evil people grow black-eyed Susans, do they?"

The hedgehog was not inclined to comment on the gardening habits of evil people.

There was a door.

It should have been a large and impressive door, perhaps something like the great carved church doors, but it wasn't. It was just a door. There was a short flight of steps, shallow and elegant, but the door at the top was dark wood, with only a little carving around the handle. The handle itself was brass, and looked no more complicated than the door handle on the burgher's door back in the village.

Rhea walked up the steps. No dead birds challenged her. Nothing jumped out of the clumps of black-eyed Susans to eat her. The stone angel did not swoop down from the fountain to carry her off, although honestly, being carried off by an angel did not seem like too terrible a fate at the moment.

She set her hand on the door knocker.

"This is a murderer's house," whispered the dead bird in her memory.

Rhea gritted her teeth and rapped the knocker sharply against the wood.

The door opened.

At first, Rhea thought the woman who had opened it was wearing some kind of high laced collar. Then she stepped back, and the light spilled over her.

Black leather thongs crossed and recrossed over the woman's throat in a tight lacing. Down the center ran a stark purple scar, a river of jagged tissue running from the underside of her chin to the hollow at her collarbone. The thongs were punched through holes in her skin, and they looked as if they had been anchored deep.

There was a long, long moment when Rhea nearly broke and ran. Never mind whatever thing had followed her down the white road, never mind Lord Crevan's rank or what he might do to her—or her parents. This was too much. Rhea's sanity was a fundamentally solid thing—she had never in fifteen years had cause to question it—but this was one shock too many, and something inside her head was whining like a beaten dog.

She took a deep breath, then another, and said in a high voice, "Lord Crevan sent for me. He—he said to come—he said this was his house—"

The woman looked at her in silence.

Rhea thrust out her hand with the silver ring on it, as if it were a token of safe passage.

The woman looked at it. She nodded, but said nothing.

Of course. She can't possibly speak, not with that scar—how did she even survive? It would be a mortal wound on anyone, a scar like that.

Maybe it was a mortal wound.

Maybe she's like the golems.

She couldn't quite deal with that thought, so she set it aside.

The woman beckoned. Her face was marked with pain and irritation, the hard lines running like knife wounds down from the sides of her nose.

"I—"

The lines deepened as the woman frowned, and she made a deeper gesture, waving Rhea inside, clearly annoyed. The hedgehog shifted restlessly in Rhea's pocket.

Rhea stepped inside.

The woman pushed the door shut behind her.

It was warmer inside, but not by very much. The door opened onto a long balcony that ran the length of another much larger room beneath it. It had to be built into the side of an unsuspected hillside, or perhaps the room had been excavated like a root cellar.

The floor below was laid with a black-and-gray checkerboard of tiles that swam before her eyes. Each tile was enormous, three feet on a side.

The silent woman gave Rhea a sharp nod and another beckoning gesture, then turned on her heel. Rhea scurried after her. The floor was carpeted with thick red rugs, and their feet made a soft sloughing sound: *uff chuff uff chuff uff chuff* . . .

She's taking me to Lord Crevan.

Oh, lord, she didn't know if she could deal with Crevan right now. She was exhausted and, she suddenly realized, ravenously hungry. The hedgehog was probably hungry, too. Of course, it would want slugs, and Lord Crevan's pantry was unlikely to have those, although if he was a sorcerer, maybe he did. Sorcerers had lots of nasty things lying around, didn't they? Slugs and bugs and worms and dragon blood and . . .

. . . *uff chuff uff chuff uff chuff.*

The woman turned down a hallway that led off the balcony.

I'm going to see him, and I'm going to babble like an idiot, or scream or cry or do something horrible. I know I am.

The silent woman stopped before a door and pulled it open. Rhea braced herself.

The room was a tiny chamber, perhaps six feet by six feet, equipped with a bed, a basin, and a small wooden chest. The woman pointed to Rhea, then to the bed, and turned to leave.

Relief struck her so strongly that she felt weak in the knees. She didn't have to face Crevan tonight. She could rest.

She was so overcome that the door had almost closed before she called, "Wait! Hang on—wait!" She pulled it open again.

The silent woman gave a tiny sigh and gazed upward, much like Rhea's mother did when praying for strength.

"I'm really hungry," said Rhea apologetically. "I didn't eat—I mean, dinner was—ah—"

The woman looked at her and shook her head—not a negative shake but a *how are you so stupid?* shake—and then turned and walked back the way they had come. Rhea hurried after her.

They went through another door, then another, and down a flight of stairs, and then they were crossing the enormous hall. The giant tiles were hard underfoot, and Rhea could feel the cold seep through the soles of her boots. The cavernous room was nearly empty, with no furniture except for an end table and a clock against the far wall. There were no paintings, no bookshelves, only dark-green walls reaching two stories overhead.

The woman was moving hurriedly now, almost running, and Rhea could barely keep up.

And then there was a noise.

It sounded like the end of the world, like the great church bell being crushed by the millstone. It was the loudest sound Rhea had ever heard. She let out a shriek and would have fallen had the silent woman not reached out and grabbed her by the scruff of the neck as if she were a kitten.

Rhea started to squirm, but the woman hauled back on her collar and dragged her close.

Then the floor fell away.

Rhea watched the stone tiles drop out of sight. They fell away into nothingness, into some dark abyss, first a few, then more and more, while that horrible grinding clangor came again and again until her very head rang with it.

The silent woman stood behind her, still holding her up by the back of her shirt, a far more solid presence than the floor. The tile they stood on was one of only a handful that remained, seemingly suspended over nothing. The walls led straight down into an enormous chasm now, wallpaper and baseboards hovering absurdly over sheer stone cliffs.

"What—how—oh, god—what—" Rhea could hear herself babbling between those terrible sounds, and then she couldn't even babble anymore and could only pant like a frightened animal.

In her pocket, the hedgehog curled into an agonizingly tight ball.

Some time later—perhaps only a few minutes, though it felt like centuries—the noise stopped.

How is this happening? Is this sorcery? What is holding us up?

And far more importantly, *How do we get down?!*

It was a very large tile, but it seemed very small with two people (and one hedgehog) standing on it. The other tiles hanging in the air were empty, except for one that carried the end table with a vase of flowers on it.

The abyss underneath was endless and very, very black.

Oh, Lady of Stones, if I fall in there, I'll have time to pray and confess my sins before I hit the bottom.

This was not a comforting thought.

"How do we get down?" whispered Rhea. She hadn't meant to whisper, but she couldn't speak any louder.

The silent woman sighed again.

Another noise began—this one a grinding, ratcheting racket, like the millworks starting up—and then a tile flew upward out of the abyss and snapped into place in absolutely empty air.

I've gone mad, said Rhea conversationally to herself. *The hedgehog was probably a warning sign. The saints only know what I've really got in my pocket.*

Another tile popped up, only a few feet beyond, and then another, and then they were all rising again, like fish surfacing in a pond when you throw bread crumbs into the water. They fitted themselves together, each of them in the right place, black bordered by gray and gray by black, and then there was a tile fitting into their tile, and another, and then the noise stopped, and the whole floor was intact.

The silent woman dropped Rhea's collar and strode out across the floor as if nothing extraordinary had happened.

It took Rhea a minute longer to gather up her courage. She put a foot on the next tile and tested it worriedly.

What if they fall?

Her guide had reached the far doorway and was waiting impatiently. How could she take a step? What if—

What if they fall again, and I'm still standing here?

Rhea crossed the vast floor in less than three seconds flat.

The silent woman snorted and pushed the door open.

Rhea stepped inside.

The room was a kitchen, built to a scale that befitted the size of the house. There was a gigantic hearth with fire irons around it and a brick oven that radiated heat. Pots and pans hung on nails overhead, and another doorway stood open, leading to what was presumably a courtyard with a pump. Cool night air drifted in through the doorway, cutting the heat from the banked hearth and the oven. (Surely the floor in here could not fall? No, of course it couldn't, there was an enormous table and a chopping block and all manner of things that would have tumbled into the abyss.)

Two women sat at the table. One was enormously fat, and the other was very pale and had a bandage wrapped around her eyes.

"Good heavens," said the fat woman, looking toward the doorway. "At this hour, too?"

"The floor," said Rhea, hearing her voice rising hysterically. "The *floor*! It—did you see—does it—it fell, and—"

"Happens every night at midnight," said the fat woman matter-of-factly. "And sometimes at a quarter after four in the afternoon, although not always. Depends on *her* mood, I should think."

"The—four in the afternoon—*her*?"

The silent woman made a wordless sound of contempt and shut the door. Rhea could hear her shoes clicking on the tiles as she strode away.

"Her," said the fat woman. "The clock wife."

Rhea said, "Oh," as if that explained things, which it didn't in the slightest.

"Have a seat, honey," said the fat woman, rising to her feet. Rhea saw that she was not merely heavy but tall as well, and powerfully built across the shoulders. "You've had a shock, and probably a long walk on top of it. Let me fry you a bit of supper."

"That would be wonderful," said Rhea, sitting down. Half her mind gibbered about the floor—everyone knew to expect little touches of magic in their lives, but the world was not a place where the floor just fell away and then came back two minutes later—and the other half had smelled bacon and was ravenously hungry and felt the floor could wait.

"Is it her?" asked the woman with the bandaged eyes. Her skin was much paler than anyone's in the village, and she had wispy white-blond hair. "Maria, is it her?"

The big woman—Maria—was chopping up a potato and tossing it into a skillet with grease and bacon.

"I'm guessing it's her, yes," said Maria. "Got Himself's ring on her finger. Ask her yourself, she's right here."

"Is she pretty, Maria?"

Rhea blinked.

Maria sighed and said, "She's young, Sylvie. Young, and not bad-looking, but she's no great beauty. Not like you were, dear." Over the frail woman's head, she mouthed, "Sorry."

Rhea wondered if she should be annoyed, and decided the potatoes were much more important.

"Oh," said Sylvie. "Oh, that's fine, then. Not that it matters." She folded her hands together, and Rhea was suddenly quite sure that it mattered *very much*.

"Egg with your potatoes, dear?"

"Oh, yes, please," said Rhea.

"Not that it matters," said Sylvie again, more loudly. And then, hesitantly, "You—you have a nice voice, dear."

"Errr. Thank you," said Rhea. She looked worriedly at Maria, who glanced at Sylvie and rolled her eyes heavenward.

"She has a nice voice," Sylvie told Maria.

"It's not nice to talk about her as if she's not here," said Maria. "What's your name, child?"

"Um. Rhea."

"Good name, that," said the fat woman approvingly. "Queen of the old gods. A strong name."

"It's important to be strong," said Sylvie. "It's better to be strong than—that is—" She stopped. Had she not been wearing the blindfold-like bandage, Rhea thought she would have been staring at her hands. "It's bad to be vain," she said finally.

She's mad, thought Rhea. *Or if not quite mad, she's at least a little touched in the head. Worse than the conjure wife anyway.*

Maria must be the cook, and I guess that means the woman with the throat wound is the butler? Maybe? And Sylvie . . . maybe she's a former servant? Or some relative of Maria's?

Would it be rude to ask? Rhea wasn't sure. If they had been in the village, she would have waited for them to volunteer the information, but if she was marrying their employer . . .

I am very tired and very hungry, and I will think about this later.

"You'll have to forgive Sylvie," said Maria, thumping a plate of potatoes, eggs, and bits of bacon down on the table in front of Rhea several moments later. "Which is not to say that she *ought* to be forgiven, but you're probably going to be here awhile, and it's just easier if we all make our peace with one another."

Rhea would have forgiven anyone anything at that point if they came bearing potatoes, but a prickly wiggling in her pocket reminded her of her manners. "Um," she said again, reaching into her skirt. "I have a hedgehog."

"So you do," said Maria, eyeing it dubiously. "I suppose it's hungry, too?"

The hedgehog managed to indicate that it could eat, yes.

Maria opened a cupboard and began rummaging through it. "I'm out of slugs," she said over her shoulder. "There are plenty out in the garden, and your services would be much appreciated there, Master—or Mistress—Hedgehog, but for now . . ."

She dumped a handful of raisins out on the table next to the hedgehog. It picked one up in its paws, nodded graciously to Maria, and tucked in.

"Useful creatures, hedgehogs," said Maria. "Is it your familiar then?"

"I don't *think* so," said Rhea, who had been applying herself to the potatoes. "We only just met. And I'm not magicky."

She glanced at the hedgehog. The hedgehog shrugged.

"Well, you never know," said Maria, wiping her hands on her apron and settling down into her chair. "I had a familiar once. Old she-bear, size of a cow by the time—well, never mind. She's still out there. Bears are nigh impossible to kill once they get to be that size. Death's too scared to come looking for them."

Sylvie stirred restlessly, as if about to say something, and Maria patted her hand firmly. The blind woman—surely she was blind?—settled back into her chair.

She had a familiar? Lord Crevan's cook had a familiar?

"So you're Rhea. Well, I'm Maria," said the cook. "And this is Sylvie, as you heard, and the grim old bat who brought you in is Ingeth."

"Are—are you Lord Crevan's servants?" asked Rhea timidly.

Maria laughed then, a rich, rollicking belly laugh that filled up the kitchen and rang the pots and pans.

"Oh, no, no, no," said Sylvie, shaking her head. Wispy hair flew.

"Bless your heart," Maria said, wiping her eyes. "Servants indeed. No, my child. We're Lord Crevan's *wives*."

Chapter Nine

"Wh-what? *Wives?*"

Maria's words meant nothing to Rhea. It was as if they had been spoken in some foreign language. People did not have more than one wife at a time. Lord Crevan was—technically—her betrothed. You didn't get betrothed to people who still had wives. Certainly not to people who had three of them!

I am very tired. I am not hearing things correctly. That's all.

"I'm sorry," said Rhea carefully, "but I think I must have misheard you."

The cook's eyes danced with a kind of jovial malice. "No, you didn't. Wives. Wives, wives, wives. As in married. As in more than one. As in me and Sylvie and Ingeth and the clock wife and the golem wife and Lady Elegans, who is lying out in the graveyard."

"Six of us," said Sylvie. "Except Lady Elegans, because she's dead. But she's still one of us. And you now of course." She sat up very straight. "You're welcome. You should be welcome. We're glad to have you. I mean, not glad that you're *here*, because that's not very nice for you, but . . ." She trailed off in some confusion, knotting her fingers together. "It's nice to have someone else to talk to," she said finally.

Maria sighed. "Poor child," she said, without any malice now. "I don't suppose you were in love with Himself, were you?"

"What?" asked Rhea blankly. Sylvie's words had filled her with vague dread. "Not very nice for you" sounded much more menacing than it should have.

"Lord Crevan," said Maria patiently. "Your husband-to-be. Himself."

"Oh! No!" Rhea shook her head. "Um. It was all very strange. He talked to my father—you can't say no to lords, not if they're wanting to marry your daughter, not if you're the miller, *you* know . . ."

Maria nodded. "Oh, aye. I know it well. Why do you think I married him? I wouldn't have set my cap for him by choice. I'd had three husbands, and his magic wasn't a patch on mine."

"You were a magician?" asked Rhea.

"I *was* a witch," said Maria, rising and busying herself around the stove. Pans clattered against each other as she moved. "Hearth and heath and heartwood. I could call the great beasts out of the earth and wire them together with silver chain." She tipped another egg onto Rhea's plate and poured out a cup of hot chocolate. "Ah, well. That was longer ago than I'd like to admit."

"You shouldn't brag," whispered Sylvie. "It isn't nice. It's vain. We can't be vain, Maria."

The blind woman's hands trembled when she spoke. Maria reached over and took her hand firmly. "Don't fret yourself, dear. It's late and he's away and we're all a bit tired. Isn't that right, Rhea?"

"Absolutely," said Rhea, who was very, very tired. The hedgehog had finished its raisins and was curled up in a small prickly ball against her plate. "Um—you said he was away?"

"Off on business," said Maria. "Nobody here but us."

"Can I leave then?" asked Rhea. "If he's not here—I was supposed to meet him—"

Hope didn't even have time to flower. Maria was already shaking her head. "Back down the white road? I wouldn't recommend it, unless you're looking for a painful death. He called up things on the white road and had neither wit nor will enough to put them down again. I don't think he knows what's down there himself." Her smile was oddly satisfied.

"I walked down here on the road . . . ," said Rhea, remembering the sensation of something on the road behind her.

"Sure," said Maria. "So did we, once. It's safe enough coming. Not so safe going, unless Himself decides to give you passage back."

I'll have to ask him for passage back. Whenever he gets here. Rhea scowled into her hot chocolate. "He told me to come, and he knew he wasn't going to be here?"

"Very like him," said Maria. "He'll set you tasks merely to prove that you have to do them." She patted Rhea's shoulder. "Best get some sleep. Ingeth!"

Ingeth appeared in the doorway moments later, looking sour. Rhea tried not to stare at the terrifying wound across her throat.

"Show Rhea here back to her room, Ingeth—and take the short way, damn you. It's late, and no one's soul is being saved tonight."

Ingeth bared her teeth at Maria. It was probably Rhea's imagination that they looked sharp. Then she turned away, jerking her head at Rhea to follow. Rhea scooped up the hedgehog and hurried after her.

The way did seem shorter, perhaps since the floor stayed where it was this time. Ingeth's back was a hard line in the dimness. She pointed to the door of Rhea's room, then turned on her heel and stalked away.

Rhea wanted time to think, but she was so tired that she fell into a dark and dreamless sleep the moment she climbed into bed.

She woke, and for a moment she could not think of where she was.

The ceiling was white, not thatch. She was in the wrong place. She had woken up, every day of her life, looking up at the thatched roof of her room (or occasionally at the beams of the mill, although sleeping near a grinding mill is not easy).

This was not thatch. It was white beadboard, thin lines and thick ones, running over her head.

What—where—why—

And then she turned her head and saw the hedgehog curled into a neat ball on the chair, and she remembered everything.

It seemed like a strange and horrible dream—the white road, the bird golems, the falling floor. Impossible to believe in the light of day. But Maria the cook, blind Sylvie—the other wives—

That Rhea could believe.

Lord Crevan already has six wives. Five, I suppose, if you don't count the dead one.

Dead wives were automatically respectable—there were widowers aplenty in the village—but not if you had five others who were alive.

And me. The seventh.

Not that I have to marry him now, do I? I mean, he already has plenty of wives!

He shouldn't even have asked me.

But he *had* asked. And if she went back home and told everyone that Lord Crevan had a half-dozen wives, a full house of them . . .

Although some of them don't quite sound real. The golem wife? What's that? And the clock wife? You can't marry a clock. Maybe he's only got the three. And the dead one.

Three living wives were not significantly better than seven. Really, any number over *none* was pretty bad.

If I could just get someone out here to meet them . . .

She chewed on her lower lip. The blankets were coarse gray wool, very clean, rough against her fingers. She scraped her fingertips over the hem, back and forth, thinking.

You'd think we would have heard that he had wives already. People would have talked. Somebody should have said something.

But nobody had. Susannah had remembered someone saying he was a widower. And that was all. People didn't know about his wives. People didn't even know he had a manor house, and given the size of the place, that was completely impossible. Somehow, Crevan was right here in the woods, with a huge house and too many wives, and nobody knew anything about it.

So what would happen if I went home and told everyone?

The hedgehog sat up and yawned.

It would be my word against his. A peasant girl against a lord. Do I expect my father to storm his house and drag out the cook and get her to testify?

And if he did, how would we get home again? If we can't go back down the white road, we'd both be trapped here. Anyone who came here to see about the wives wouldn't be able to leave again, unless Crevan let them.

It was hard to make herself believe that she was trapped. She had only Maria's word for it after all, and she'd only known the cook for a couple of hours.

Well, Maria's word, and the way that the hedgehog was acting . . .

Rhea frowned. She trusted the hedgehog, despite how mad that sounded. And it had been afraid to go back down the white road.

There's something out there. And that means I can't leave unless he lets me.

Her fingers tightened on the blankets.

No. No, he has to let me go home. People will notice if I don't come back. And if I go home, I could go to the viscount and . . .

She thought of what was likely to happen if she did. Even if she managed to prove it, the mill would undoubtedly change hands. Viscount Skeller would not react well to someone who embarrassed a peer of his. Even if that person was absolutely in the right. And when the time came to renew the leases—the leases that had been a mere formality for generations—

Rhea sat up. Her heart was a dragging weight in her chest. Nothing had changed.

She was still going to get married.

It was just going to be worse than she had thought.

Chapter Ten

She tucked the hedgehog into her pocket and went downstairs, finding her way to the kitchen by following the smell of bread baking. The black-and-gray tile floor was quiet underfoot. She stamped her foot on a tile, and it felt as solid as the foundations of the mill.

The clock squatted in a corner of the hall, as wide as the altar of the village church and twice as tall. A glass door enclosed the mechanism, which looked, to Rhea's practiced eye, rather like a dozen interlocking mill wheels.

No one in town had a clock like this. Big clocks were expensive. Water clocks and marked hour candles were still more common in town. She'd never met anyone who could afford to buy a clock from the rat speaker in Barrelridge.

She wondered if this clock was one of his, but upon a closer look, she thought not. The gears were small, but still on a scale made by humans, not by rats.

At the moment, the hands stood at nine thirty, comfortably far off from midnight. Also nowhere near four in the afternoon.

Maria said something about a clock wife. Is this what she meant?

Lord Crevan can't have married a clock. *That's . . . I mean . . . normal people don't marry clocks.*

Of course, normal people don't marry seven wives at a time, either. Normal people don't marry fifteen-year-old peasant girls.

Rhea scowled. Her reflection in the glass scowled back.

Maybe that wife makes clocks. That doesn't explain the thing with the floor, but . . .

Is there anything *that could explain the thing with the floor?*

Magic, in Rhea's experience, was a small thing—gremlins, hollyhocks, and rogue vegetables. Floors that fell away like the tile floor had done seemed too large to be magic. It was more like a storm or an earthquake or some other force of nature.

Then again, if Crevan's hiding a manor out here, who knows what sort of magic he can use?

For the life of her, though, Rhea could not figure out how making the floor fall away would be of any use to a sorcerer.

She turned to go, and something caught her eye. What had looked like two hands shifted, just slightly, and she realized that there was a third hand behind the others.

It was perfectly clear and glittered like ice. Rhea leaned in until her breath steamed on the glass, but could not see it moving.

. . . huh.

"You're up early," said Maria as Rhea entered the kitchen. "I expected you to sleep the sun round."

Rhea shrugged.

"Oh, to be young again," said the cook. "Well, you're here now, so you can make yourself useful. Eggs and potatoes again?"

"Yes, please."

"Good." Maria slid a pair of shears across the scarred tabletop. "Go out in the garden and cut a bouquet of herbs, and it'll be done when you are."

"What sort of herbs do you need?" asked Rhea.

"Anything that smells strongly," said Maria. "They're for Sylvie. She can't see flowers anymore, so we make do." She smiled faintly. "They don't even have to smell completely good, just so long as she can smell them."

Rhea nodded and slipped out the door into the garden.

High walls surrounded the garden, though an archway stood open and ungated. The wood pressed up close against the house here, and over the tops of the walls, Rhea could see branches. Some of the boughs were weighed down with apples.

An overgrown orchard, then. Judging by the shapes of the trees, nobody had tended it for a long time.

It looked as if Aunt was mistaken, and there would be no army of servants. Rhea took some small, grumpy satisfaction in that fact.

It was a damp morning. Fog hung in tatters from the trees. The kitchen garden was organized in squares, with broad rows of radishes and cabbages and lettuce. Herbs stood in a wheel at the center.

She edged forward so she could have a better look out the archway. The leaves lay thick under the apple trees, the ground choked with grass and brambles.

She let the hedgehog out of her pocket, and it immediately trundled off into the beds. "I'll . . . um . . . come back for you later?" Rhea called.

The hedgehog nodded over its shoulder to her.

Well, it'll take care of any slugs they may have, I suppose . . .

She cut the bouquet carefully, taking her time among the herbs. Rosemary of course, and a short length of oregano. Hyssop and fennel. One late rose, missing half its petals but still producing a sweet, rounded fragrance. The rest had gone to rose hips. She wrapped it all in some thin stems of chickweed, which smelled like nothing except green.

Rhea went back inside. Maria looked over her bouquet and nodded approval. "Good. The chickweed's a nice touch. She won't know that one right off, and it'll make her happy guessing."

"Shall I cut off the thorns?" asked Rhea. "So Sylvie doesn't prick herself?"

Maria shook her head. "Roses have thorns," she said. "That's the price of roses. When you start to forget that, that's when things go wrong." She set Rhea's breakfast down in front of her, and Rhea ate it slowly, trying to figure out what that meant and if there was any message she could take away from it.

She eventually decided there wasn't. She scraped the last bits of egg yolk up on the side of her fork. "Are there many people here to cook for?"

Maria shook her head. She was pummeling dough into submission. "No more than you've seen. The golem wife don't eat, and the clock wife can't. Himself comes out every few months, and he don't mind plain cooking while he's here."

Rhea looked up, startled. "Every few months? Where is he the rest of the time?"

"In the city, child," said Maria. Flour rose up in great gusts as she slapped the dough against the board. "The capital city, with the king and the queen and all the court. He comes out here to do his experiments and play with his magic. There's little enough here to interest him but solitude."

Rhea digested this. Did that mean that if she married him, she would be expected to go into the capital with him? Or that she would be staying here, in this house?

The notion of being stuck in this house with Maria and Ingeth and Sylvie and whatever horrible thing was going on with the tile floor was not terribly appealing.

On the other hand, a husband who wasn't around . . . well, he couldn't expect her to do . . . things. The sort of things that led to babies. Rhea knew perfectly well what those things entailed and had a certain intellectual curiosity about them, but she couldn't picture doing them with an older man who'd admitted to being a sorcerer.

It occurred to her that if he had a great many wives, Lord Craven had probably done *those* things with Marie and Sylvie and grim Ingeth.

She felt her face get hot, and buried that thought as fastidiously as a cat burying its own droppings.

"Is he going to stay away for months this time, do you think?"

That wouldn't be so bad. She could stay for a few days, then make her apologies and go home. Though she couldn't take the white road, there had to be another way. She was needed at the mill. He hadn't married her yet. Somebody had to thump the hopper and check for gremlins.

And if he doesn't come back, I can leave. Go somewhere. Go anywhere.

My parents can tell him that I died, and then he won't be angry with them and there won't be questions and it won't all end with the viscount taking away the mill. I can run as far away as I need to.

It has to be better than being trapped here forever.

"Not hardly," said Maria. "He'll be back before long. There's a bag of sugar and a gallon of cream in the pantry."

Rhea raised her eyebrows.

"We get deliveries regular," said Maria. "A lad with a cart, and don't ask me what road he takes to get here, 'cause I don't believe it's a canny one. Still, Himself won't let us starve out here, though we do run a bit low on the luxuries if he's in town for the season." She jerked her chin toward the pantry door. "But we've been getting the good stuff, and that means he'll be here for a few weeks. He don't expect me to produce roast peacock, but he wants white flour and clotted cream at least."

"Oh," said Rhea.

Her hopes hadn't risen far enough to dash. She sighed.

"There's dishes in the scullery need washing," said Maria. "Is a miller's daughter too good to wash dishes?"

Rhea shook her head. "I can wash dishes. I'm better with milling, though."

"No mill out here. We get the flour already ground." She tossed Rhea an apron. It hung most of the way to the floor, and Rhea had to weave the ties around herself twice. Maria shook her head. "Well, since you'll be staying, we'll see about sewing up some new clothes for you. Sylvie was a dab hand at it, when she could see, but now . . ."

"It's okay," said Rhea. "I'm sure I don't need them. I mean—not yet." The notion of getting new clothes filled her with immediate dread. New clothes for this place meant that she really was staying.

Maria put a hand on her shoulder and squeezed. It was brief and comforting, the weight of the woman's large forearm as heavy as a hug. "As you wish, child. As you wish."

Dishes for three people did not take long to wash. Rhea hung up the apron and went back into the kitchen.

"May I look around?" she asked timidly. "The house, I mean?" She was not sure why she was asking Maria, except that the cook had an air of authority.

"Do as you like," said Maria. "You might as well know where everything is."

Rhea did not linger in the tiled hall for long. She thought she remembered which tiles were safe, but she did not want to put it to the test.

She crossed the hall and went up the staircase, into the hallway.

There were doorways on both sides. The door to her bedroom was ajar, which was the only reason that she recognized it.

She laid her hand on the doorknob of the door next to it.

If I married Lord Crevan, I'd be the lady of the manor, wouldn't I? These rooms would belong to me.

Well. One *of the ladies of the manor, apparently.*

Perhaps they'd all share ownership of the manor, or perhaps they'd each get a set of rooms and a chunk of hallway.

One-seventh of the tiles in the great hall, one-seventh of the bedrooms, one-seventh of the attics—assuming there are attics—

She snorted to herself, not sure if she was angry or amused, and pushed the door open.

It was a room identical to her bedroom—small, whitewashed, with a basin on a stand.

The next three rooms were also identical. The fourth was twice the size, with two narrow beds on either side of the room.

Oh, look. Housing for wives eight, nine, and ten . . . and I suppose eleven and twelve will be twins . . .

She abandoned the row of doors and followed the hall around the corner, back toward the main entrance. The doorways became fewer and larger, with paintings hanging between them.

It was too dim to make out any detail in the paintings—hunting scenes, she thought. Horses and hounds and a blur of paint that might be a fox.

Rhea opened one of the large doorways.

The ballroom beyond was not as large as the great hall, but it was completely empty. Not even one piece of furniture broke up the severe lines of the walls. She took two steps inside, and her footsteps echoed so jarringly that she stepped back onto the carpet at once.

The dust lay thick on the floor. She could see her footprints in it.

If someone opens this door, they'll know I've been here.

And that means . . . what, exactly? There's no crime in looking at an empty ballroom, is there?

She could not shake the feeling that she was trespassing somehow, in the empty silence of the house.

There was a smaller doorway opposite the ballroom. It was locked.

Huh.

The next three doors were also locked, and Rhea wondered what lay behind them. Something Crevan valued? A place where a sorcerer did his magic?

For all I know, it's Ingeth's bedroom and she doesn't want me checking in to see if she made her bed.

She had gotten used to the locks and was surprised when the next doorknob turned easily under her hand.

It was a room, smaller than the ballroom, but not empty. Sheets were draped over the furniture. Some of the shapes were easy to work out—a flat-topped square was a table, and that one there was a chair—but others were cryptic under their sheets.

It was all too easy to imagine someone hiding in there, crouched down under a sheet.

How would you ever know?

She closed the door and wiped her hands on her skirts.

The next room was a dining hall. The table was vast and could seat forty. The chair at the head of the table was the size of a throne. Wrought-iron candlesticks in the shapes of horses reared over the center of the table.

It smelled of neglect and mouse nests. The edges of the tablecloth had been chewed by moths.

"It is clear," said Rhea, out loud because the silence was weighing on her, "that Lord Crevan does not entertain often."

Well. He wouldn't, would he? Someone might find out about all those wives.

Us wives.

She closed the door to the dining room and found that she was less interested in what might lie behind the other doors.

As she was walking through the hallway, back toward her room, she heard a sound.

If the silence in the house had not been so absolute, she would have missed it. It was muffled by doors and layers of carpet, but nevertheless she could hear . . . something.

The wall it seemed to emanate from was unbroken. She had to follow the noise down the stairs and under them, through another hallway, before she found a doorway.

She expected it to be locked, but it was not.

It was a perfectly ordinary room. There was no furniture in it. There was only dust on the floor—and tracks in the dust.

The noise came again.

It was a tapping. Someone was knocking on the far wall, from the other side—and yet it didn't sound quite like a fist against wood.

"Ingeth?" said Rhea aloud. "Is that you?"

There was no answer. The tapping paused.

She walked forward. The footprints led to the wall, ending to one side of where Rhea herself now stood.

The tap came again, under her ear. It was not a threatening sound. It sounded like the knocking that happened in the mill when one of the slats came loose and the vibration made it bang against the hopper.

"Is someone there?"

It stopped.

Rhea waited for another minute or two, but it did not resume.

She followed the footprints back out the door.

It took her several minutes, walking back and forth, but she eventually determined that there was no hidden bedroom on the other side of that wall.

In fact, if I am not completely turned around—and I might be, because these hallways have too many turns—I think that the other side of that wall is about . . . here.

She stood in the tiled hall. In front of her was the clock.

Chapter Eleven

At dinner, Rhea summoned the courage to ask, "Why does Lord Crevan get six wives?"

Sylvie turned her head toward Rhea's voice. Ingeth glared, her drawstring mouth drawing tighter.

All four of them were eating in the kitchen. Rhea thought of the dining room, with its long table and dusty cushions. She could not picture eating there, like a great lady.

Or four great ladies, assuming we're all his wives . . .

"Look around," said Maria. "Who's going to stop him?"

"But—I mean—*legally*—"

"Laws for the gentry aren't laws for us," said Maria. "You know that, child."

"But that can't be right," said Rhea. "I mean—yes, okay, obviously. Most laws, sure. But they don't let the *king* have six wives." She paused, scowling down at her mashed potatoes. "Well . . . not all at the same time anyway."

Ingeth pushed her food away and walked out of the room.

"Don't mind her," said Maria. "She's still angry for being taken in." She gestured with a piece of bread. "Think it through. A king can't have six wives, but if a peasant girl turned up and swore she'd been married to the king in a secret ceremony, how far do you think she'd get?"

Rhea nodded glumly.

Well, it was no more than she'd worked out for herself. Although—

"Why does he *want* six wives?"

"Bit of a collector, isn't he?" the cook said, and snickered.

Rhea felt the tips of her ears grow hot.

"Don't tease," said Sylvie suddenly. "He married us because he knew he could make better use of our gifts than we could."

Rhea blinked.

"Don't start that crap again, Sylvie—"

"Oh, but we deserved it!" said the blind woman, nodding.

"Hush," said the cook heavily.

"We did! When did we do anything of use with our gifts? I was vain, so vain, like a young peacock. I spent hours before my mirror. And what did Ingeth ever do with her voice but pray and sermonize at all hours until she drove everyone half mad around her?"

"They were *our* failings," said Maria. She stood up and began slamming down pans. "Our gifts to waste or not, as we chose. Whether we used them well or not, he had no right to be judge, jury, and executioner."

Maria dropped a cast-iron pan on the stove. Sylvie flinched. Her shoulders shook, and she made a small, thin noise into her hands.

It took Rhea a few minutes to realize that the other woman was crying. Wet splotches formed on the cloth over her eyes.

She sat there awkwardly. Should she get up and comfort Sylvie? Would the gesture be welcomed, or would it only embarrass her?

"Hey," she said softly. "Hey—um—"

Sylvie didn't seem to hear her.

"Hey—Sylvie—uh—"

The cook turned around and sighed. "Oh, hell. Sylvie, I'm sorry."

"We *must* have deserved it," said Sylvie. "Oh, Maria, we must have! It wouldn't have been allowed otherwise."

"Allowed by who?" asked Maria. "The king? The priest? Ingeth's picky little god? None of them know what goes on in this house."

Sylvie looked around, her white-blond hair hanging in wisps. "Maria, don't—please don't yell."

The cook's expression softened, and she put an arm around the other woman. "Hush, Sylvie, don't cry. I'm in a bad mood because he's done it again. I shouldn't take it out on you."

Rhea had a pretty good idea that "he's done it again" also meant "and she's sitting here at the table." She twisted her fingers together. The silver ring was cold.

He makes better use of our gifts than we can? What does that mean? What gifts? Is this a magic thing? But what do staring into the mirror and sermonizing have to do with magic?

For that matter, Ingeth had been sermonizing? This must have been before her terrible throat wound. What had happened to her?

Sylvie leaned her head against Maria's large shoulder and sighed. It did not seem like a good time to be asking questions. Rhea took her empty plate into the scullery and left the other wives alone.

She was halfway through the dirty dishes when the house shook.

It was not the sickening shaking that had accompanied the falling floor. It was only a little stillness, and then the whole building shuddered once, as if someone had walked across its grave. A little dust slipped from the beams overhead and pattered across the clean dishes.

I'll have to re-rinse those plates, thought Rhea, annoyed, and then, belatedly, *the house shook again.*

Perhaps she was getting used to it. What a vile thought.

Maria stuck her head in the scullery door and said, "Himself's home."

Rhea paused with her hands full of plates. "Should I go to my room and change?" She was wearing her second-best skirt, which was gray and shapeless and comfortable. The red dress was still in her pack, probably full of wrinkles.

The cook snorted. "And then you'll be waiting and fretting and the dishes will still need to get done. No, best stay busy. He'll keep you waiting awhile, just so you know he's in charge."

Not, thought Rhea grimly, *that I'm likely to forget* that.

Maria was right. She had finished the dishes and was pulling off her apron when Ingeth appeared at the kitchen door.

She jerked her chin at Rhea.

Rhea glanced at Maria. The cook dipped her head and said, "Courage, child. But not too much. He plans to break you, and it'll go easier for you if you bend."

Ingeth glowered. In Rhea's mind, the bird golems whispered, "Be bold, be bold, but not too bold . . ."

She wiped her hands on the sides of her skirt and wished that she still had the hedgehog with her.

Sylvie smiled in Rhea's general direction. The blind woman probably meant to be encouraging, but Rhea could only read her expression as sad.

"Mind the floor," called Maria. "The clock wife likes to drop it when Himself's in residence. Hopes she'll catch him, but she hasn't yet."

Too bad, thought Rhea.

She followed Ingeth out of the kitchen.

They went up the grand staircase. Rhea gripped the polished banister. It was too slippery to be of much use as a support, but it was a solid thing in a house where even the floors weren't particularly solid.

Ingeth did not pause at the top of the stairs, and Rhea had to scurry after her.

The carpet here was even thicker and softer than it was outside Rhea's bedroom. Their feet made no sound at all.

A series of portraits lined the hallway. She looked up into one painted face after another. Some were cruel, some were kind. A few weren't human. There was one of an eagle wearing a crown, and the eagle's painted eyes were as thoughtful and intelligent as those of the human man opposite him.

Be bold, be bold, but not too bold . . . , thought Rhea.

Ingeth stopped at a door and tapped at it, very lightly. Then she crossed her arms over her breast and stepped back.

"Enter," called Lord Crevan through the door.

Rhea looked at Ingeth, but Ingeth sank her chin to her chest and did not look at her.

Though it was the very last thing she wanted to do, Rhea gulped and opened the door.

The room inside was paneled in dark wood. Presumably there was furniture, but it was so dim that Rhea could barely make out any shapes. The carpet muffled her footsteps.

There was a single narrow window on the right-hand wall, and a reading stand with a heavy book on it was angled just so to capture the muted beam of light it cast. Lord Crevan stood in front of the book, turning the pages one by one.

"Rhea," he said, looking up.

"Milord," Rhea said, and managed a real curtsey this time.

He smiled. She didn't like the look of it. It was the same smile he had worn when the spark had jumped from his hand to hers—the smug smile of a man who believes he is the smartest person in the room, and has just done something unspeakably clever.

Well. Perhaps he had.

"What do you think of my house, Miss Rhea?"

She did not like the "miss." It had a note of mockery in it.

"It is very large," she said.

"And what do you think of my wives?" he asked.

Well.

Apparently they were not going to dance around the topic at all.

Rhea bit back her anger. It was easy, because under and over and shot through her anger was fear. She had only to summon up her father's face and think of the mill. Lord Crevan had already taken her away from her family. She would be damned if he got an excuse to take the mill away as well.

Besides, she didn't want to give him the satisfaction of seeing her react.

"Maria and Sylvie have been very welcoming," she said quietly.

The skin around his eyes tightened, just a little. If she had not been staring at his face, she might have missed it. "Good," he said. "Very good. I want you to feel at home here."

Was it her imagination, or did he sound the tiniest bit disappointed?

They faced each other in silence. He turned another page of the book on the stand, without looking down at it, then another.

Eventually, because someone had to say something, Rhea said, "Thank you for inviting me."

"Naturally."

"When may I return home, milord?"

His smug smile returned and settled. "Are you so eager to leave, Miss Rhea?"

"My family will miss me," said Rhea, which was undoubtedly true.

"Ah . . ." He steepled his fingers. "And yet they have had you your entire life—what is it, fourteen years?"

"Fifteen."

"As long as that? Well then. But I have had you only a day. They will have to get on without you a little longer."

Rhea dropped her gaze to hide her disappointment. She had not expected him to let her go so easily. Truly she hadn't. But it still felt as if he had set his boot in the middle of her chest and pushed.

When she looked again, he had turned partly away and was reading through the book. "There is something you might do for me, while you are here," he said.

"Milord?"

"There is a place in the woods. Follow the path out through the gardens and the old orchard, and at the end of it is a clearing with a pool and a . . . ah . . . *scarecrow.*" He did not look up. "Give the scarecrow a drink from the pool, then return."

"A scarecrow that drinks water, milord?"

He smiled down at the book. "Leave at moonrise," he said after a moment. "Return before dawn, or you will have failed."

"Failed, milord?" Rhea concentrated on keeping her voice even.

Failed? If I don't come back before dawn? Failed how? Is this magic, or is he simply mad?

"Failed," said Lord Crevan. "And there is a price for failure, Miss Rhea. Come back before dawn, or else I'll marry you."

Chapter Twelve

Rhea had to find her way back alone. Ingeth was still standing outside the door, her arms crossed, but when Rhea asked her for directions to her room, the other woman gave her a look of such intense loathing that it struck her like a physical blow.

She was too tired to deal with it now. She turned away and walked back up the hallway, feeling Ingeth's stare on the back of her neck.

The stairway down was at the end of the hall. Presumably her own room was somewhere else in the house, but she wasn't sure how to get there. At least the kitchen was half familiar.

Maria turned as she came through the door, took one look at her, and hooked a chair out with her foot. "Sit down, child. You're looking rough."

Rough. Yes. Rough describes it well. She felt as worn as a rutted road.

She collapsed into the chair, and without being asked, Maria brought her a mug of tea and a jar of honey. Rhea drizzled honey into the tea, watching the thin thread of amber cross and recross itself before sinking into the depths of the mug.

It seemed very important to watch the honey.

Sylvie cleared her throat. Rhea hadn't noticed her in the room. The blind woman stood in the doorway to the garden, holding the door-frame. "Maria?" she asked quietly.

"I'm here," said Maria. "It's only Rhea. She's come from an audience with Himself and she's a bit shook up is all."

"Oh," said Sylvie. She hovered in the doorway, then walked, setting her feet carefully one in front of the other, to her usual chair at the table. "My bouquet was lovely," she said, turning her head in Rhea's direction. "I didn't guess the chickweed at all. I never thought of it."

"It's a weed, mostly," said Rhea, who would much rather think of chickweed than of husbands. "You have to pull it up by the handfuls in the garden back home, and afterward your hands smell . . . green. I don't know how else to describe it."

Sylvie nodded. "Like spring," she said. "Before any of the flowers do anything, and everything is just leaves and stems." She folded her hands neatly on the table in front of her. "Though it's autumn now."

Rhea nodded and then remembered that Sylvie couldn't see it, and said, "Yes."

She took a sip from the mug of tea. She had added too much honey, but she drank it anyway.

Maria sat down in her own chair and thumped her elbows onto the table. "All right," she said. "What did Himself want?"

Rhea stared into her tea and felt her ability to pretend that the conversation with Lord Crevan had never happened slipping away.

I'm not going to cry. Crying is stupid. I already cried on the road. I don't want to cry in front of Sylvie and Maria.

"I have to go out tonight," she said. "To find a scarecrow and give it a drink of water."

"Scarecrow." Maria's lip curled. "Is that what she is now?"

Sylvie made a restless motion, her hands fluttering against the scarred wood of the table.

Maria glanced at her and exhaled. "Very well. If that's the way it is, that's the way it is."

Rhea was reminded, suddenly, of her mother and aunt trying to build a net of words around the indecency of her visit to Lord Crevan.

She wanted to yell, "What is *really* going on here?!" because it was obvious that *something* was. Nobody sent you out in the middle of the night to give a scarecrow a drink of water. It was insane.

It was as insane as walking along a white road and meeting bird golems that whispered to you in hollow voices. It was as insane as a tile floor that dropped out from under you at midnight.

It was as insane as a miller's daughter marrying a lord who was also a sorcerer.

She glanced at Maria, who had once been a witch. Of all of them, Maria would know what was going on.

But when she opened her mouth to demand answers, Maria locked gazes with her and shook her head, her lips pressed into a flat line.

Rhea did not want to be silenced. But Maria flicked her eyes to the ceiling, in the general direction of Crevan's study, then back down to Rhea. She shook her head again.

Rhea closed her mouth.

Sylvie, who could undoubtedly feel the tension, plucked at the table again. "She wasn't bad-looking," she murmured. "Her hair was nice."

"Hush, Sylvie."

Rhea finished her tea.

"You'll find the road easy enough," said Maria. "It's returning that's the tricky part. What time are you to leave?"

"Moonrise," said Rhea.

"Aye. Himself is fond of moonrise." She pushed herself to her feet. "All right then. You should take a nap. It'll be a long night, and moonrise will come sooner than you think."

* * *

Rhea slept.

She wouldn't have thought it possible. The sheets were cool, and she drifted first into a vague half sleep, full of white walls and silence, and then into dreaming.

In that dark manor, she would have expected nightmares. And yet, when she dreamed, it was of the mill and the stream flowing past. Only ordinary things. There were no swans in the water, no monsters in the shadows.

Well, she thought, half waking, *I am living in some evil dream already. There would hardly be any point to nightmares.*

It was after dark when Ingeth knocked on the door.

The other woman's scarred throat was a shock to Rhea's sleep-dazed eyes. She woke up in a hurry. "I—wait—oh. Yes. Let me get my shoes on."

Ingeth glared through her, then turned on her heel and stalked away.

Rhea hurried after her, with the back of one shoe still crumpled up under her foot. When she reached the kitchen, she flopped down in a chair to fix her shoe. She could see the garden through the door, and while it was bathed in starlight, the moon had not yet risen.

"There you are," said Maria, elbow deep in bread dough. "I sent Ingeth to wake you. You'll need a meal before you go out."

Out. Yes. Into the woods. At night.

Rhea's stomach knotted up. She dragged her finger around the back of her shoe, flipping the leather up. "Oh. I suppose that's a good idea."

I did it once before. I was fine. I had a hedgehog. I'll be fine this time, too.

She wondered if the hedgehog was waiting in the garden for her. She hoped it was.

"It's a very good idea," said Maria. "It'll be bad enough without being hungry, I expect."

This was not precisely encouraging.

"What's going to happen to me?" asked Rhea.

"I was a witch, not a fortune-teller," said Maria testily. "No one knows what's going to happen."

She slid a plate of potatoes in front of Rhea, then returned to the dough. Potatoes seemed to be Maria's default food. Fortunately, Rhea was fond of them.

She wasn't exactly hungry, but she took a bite anyway.

Sylvie was not at the table. Rhea looked over her shoulder to make sure Ingeth was gone.

"Maria?"

"Mm?"

"Why does Ingeth hate me?"

Maria let out a bark of laughter. "She was the last wife. Voice like an angel, and what did she ever use it for but picking and picking and telling us that we had led our lord to wickedness. She thought she'd had the saving of him, what with her sermons and her righteousness, and then she got here and found he had five other wives and only one in the ground."

Rhea could spare a certain amount of sympathy for Ingeth's surprise. "She didn't know?"

"No more than the rest of us. Well, not me. I was the first wife." She slammed her fist into the dough, perhaps with a little more force than needed. "Hard for someone like Ingeth to admit she was wrong. Or maybe she's mad at her god for not saving her. I don't know. It's quieter now, thank the saints."

"What happened to her?" asked Rhea quietly.

Maria looked up at the ceiling, then down at Rhea.

I should have asked before. Oh, it was stupid not to ask when I first got here. They were talking freely then. I was tired and scared and upset, but that's still no excuse. She can't talk with Lord Crevan here, it's obvious. He has some way of hearing us.

Lady of Stones, why was I so stupid?

In a very small voice, Rhea said, "He told me that if I'm not back before dawn, he'll marry me."

Maria nodded. She came over and took the half-eaten plate of potatoes away. When her lips were very near Rhea's ear, she murmured, "I can't say much. But I'd be back by dawn if I were you."

Chapter Thirteen

When the edge of the moon slithered over the top of the wood, Rhea stepped into the garden, onto the path that continued through the archway, into the overgrown garden, into the orchard, and then . . . well, hopefully to the scarecrow.

The scarecrow that could drink.

She took a deep breath to settle herself. The air smelled of dead leaves and frost.

Rhea made three steps, and then a shadow waddled into the path. The hedgehog sat up in front of her.

"Hedgehogs are not this concerned with humans," Rhea told it firmly as a wave of relief washed through her like a cool tide.

The hedgehog shrugged and put its paws in the air to be picked up.

She settled it into her pocket, where it rolled around until it found a comfortable position. "Were the slugs in the garden good?" she asked it.

It poked its nose over the pocket edge and nodded approvingly. Apparently, they had been high-quality slugs.

She told the hedgehog about her errand as she walked out of the garden. The path was pale in the moonlight, but it was nothing like the bone-colored expanse of the white road. When leaves fell over it, they lay like ordinary leaves, and not like blood.

The orchard was heavy and overgrown. Weeds turned to brambles and grew up the trunks of apples, which bent branches down to meet them. The path became narrower the deeper she went, but it was still six paces across and mostly straight.

This isn't so bad. If this is all there is, I shouldn't have any trouble getting home by dawn.

The fallen leaves cluttered the edges, but the center of the path stayed clear.

Rhea looked over her shoulder. She had no sense of anything following her, but she didn't entirely trust her senses. She looked down at the hedgehog.

Its tiny paws were tense, but it did not seem afraid.

They had been walking no more than fifteen or twenty minutes when the dense tangle swept away on either side and Rhea stepped into a clearing.

The moon streamed down on grass-choked paving stones. The gaps where stones were missing were scabbed with weeds.

Tall wooden poles were sunk in the ground at random, like flagpoles. A few had crosspieces on them, lashed with rope. Rhea could see no purpose for them.

I suppose you could run a cord between them and dry your laundry.

Some people grow vines up a pole. They could have been used for roses or grapes or something. They're too big for beanpoles.

But it did not look as if anything had grown up the poles for a long, long time.

She edged farther into the clearing. The stones were deeply sunk into the earth and did not move underfoot.

There was a depression on the far side of the clearing—the pool. Black trees were reflected in the water, along with a faint dusting of stars.

In her pocket, the hedgehog shifted uneasily.

The stones were hard underfoot, and the edges dug into the soles of her boots. Rhea carefully picked her way across the clearing.

"There's supposed to be a scarecrow here . . . ," she said aloud. The words made a little space that belonged to her, not to the dark trees and strange poles. She kept talking, to herself or the hedgehog, she wasn't sure. "I suppose it could be gone. How long do scarecrows last? It would serve Lord—*Himself* right."

She avoided Lord Crevan's name at the last minute. Suddenly it seemed safer to use Maria's term out here, where things might be listening.

"He called up things on the white road and had neither wit nor will enough to put them down again," Maria had said.

Rhea had no idea where the white road was in relation to this clearing. Surely it was in the same woods, somewhere nearby?

How far could a monster travel? Could something walk off the white road, slither through the woods, and devour—oh, to take an example completely at random—an unwary girl and her hedgehog?

"Can't think like that," muttered Rhea. "Otherwise, I'll turn around and run back to the house, and then he'll marry me."

The hedgehog shivered, and she felt a sudden prickle of spines through her skirt before it settled down.

Rhea reached the edge of the pool.

The stones had sunk here—not as if they had fallen away, but as if the earth had subsided under them. The pool had leaves at the bottom, and moss grew luxuriantly along the edges.

If she had been here during the day, it might have been a pleasant place.

She raised her eyes and saw what could only be the scarecrow.

The hedgehog rolled itself into a ball as Rhea flung herself backward. Her ankle caught on something, and she fell on her backside. Her breath was driven out in a great startled *whuff!*

All she could think was *Of course, of course, I should have known it wouldn't be a real scarecrow, it would be something horrible, why didn't I guess—*

It was a golem.

Like the bird golems on the arches, it was a hard, leathery thing, its skin held together with stitching. Its ribs had been broken down the middle and sewn up again so that the breastbone sank inward, and its bony wrists were lashed to the cross brace of one of the poles.

Its eyes were closed. That was the only mercy. It would have been bad enough if it had stones for eyes like the bird golems, but if it had human eyes, Rhea thought she might have gone mad right there and run gibbering and whooping into the woods, never mind Lord Crevan or anyone else.

This isn't happening. That is not a real person. It wasn't ever a real person. It wasn't alive. It's just a doll or a statue or something. It has to be.

She closed her eyes and then snapped them open immediately, because what if it was like the bird golems and it *moved?*

"Shouldn't have thought that," she said under her breath. "Stupid thing to think. It's not moving. It's not alive. It's just a horrible . . . scarecrow. That's all. He told you it was a scarecrow."

The hedgehog uncurled itself and climbed out onto her chest. She looked down at it. It looked back up at her.

"This is bad," she said.

The hedgehog nodded.

Rhea flopped backward and lay flat on her back on the stones. It was not at all comfortable, but getting up again seemed like an unspeakable effort. If she watched down the side of her nose, she could see the golem hanging, unmoving, on a pole.

"A golem person," she said hoarsely. "If he made it out of a dead body, that's . . . that's really bad."

The hedgehog nodded again.

"But not as bad as if he made it out of . . ."

She stopped because saying it out loud wouldn't help one bit. The hedgehog glanced over its shoulder.

"This is a murderer's house . . . ," the bird golem had said.

Could he have killed someone and turned them into a golem? Presumably that's what he had done with the birds . . . How did you even *make* golems like that?

It suddenly occurred to her that Maria had known. "Scarecrow. Is that what she is now?" the other woman had said.

"Oh, Lady of Stones," said Rhea in a high voice. "It's the golem wife."

Chapter Fourteen

Eventually she got up, because lying on the ground wouldn't help anything.

Rhea would have sworn that nothing in the world would make her approach the golem wife. She would have sworn by the saints and the bones of her not-yet-deceased parents.

She would have been wrong.

I have to give her water. Otherwise I'll fail, and if he marries me, I could end up like her.

She thought of the other wives—blind Sylvie and throat-wounded Ingeth and the dead one in the garden. There was nothing too obvious wrong with Maria, but what did Rhea know? The cook could be concealing anything under her apron—and hadn't she said that she used to be a witch?

He does something horrible to each of them. He must. That's what Sylvie was getting at when she talked about him using their gifts—oh, Lady of Stones! What is he going to do to me?

Her heart pounded wildly, which was stupid, because Lord Crevan wasn't even there. *I'm sitting in a clearing in the woods, and the only things here are a hedgehog and a dead woman tied to a pole. Nothing's going to eat me. If I do this and get home in time, he won't marry me.*

She wiped her hands on her skirt and scooped up the hedgehog. "All right," she croaked. Her voice sounded as if she'd been crying, even though she hadn't. "All right, let's do this, and get back before morning."

The golem wife hung mutely on her pole and said nothing.

Rhea waded into the pool.

Her feet were immediately soaked. Her boots were sturdy, but not particularly waterproof, and the bottom was slick with rotted leaves. She tucked her skirt up, mindful of the hedgehog, and stepped slowly toward the golem wife.

She had a bad moment when she realized that she would have to cup the water with her bare hands. *I should have brought a cup. Well. All right. He didn't say how much water to give her.*

It occurred to her that she would have to touch the golem wife's lips with her hand. Her stomach clenched.

Suddenly the potatoes she'd eaten for dinner did not seem like such a good idea after all.

She halted in front of the golem wife.

Thick cords bound the golem's wrists to the pole. The wrists were impossibly thin, no more substantial than bone covered with hard skin. The cords looked strong and unfrayed by comparison.

She's tied up. She's tied to the pole. She can't reach out and grab me.

Rhea swallowed hard.

"Do you suppose her eyes are going to open?" she asked the hedgehog. Her voice was shaking terribly.

The hedgehog gave her a look.

"Yeah," said Rhea sadly. "Me, too."

She took a deep breath and said, in as conversational a tone as she could manage, "If you're still alive—or sort of alive—and you're going to talk like the bird golems or open your eyes, I'd rather you do it now and get it over with please."

There was a rustling that was almost like the wind, but not quite. Slowly, jerkily, the golem wife's head moved.

Her eyes slid open.

They were black river rocks, the same as the bird golems' had been. Rhea let out a shuddering breath.

In a way it was a relief. She had known it was going to happen after all, and it would have been much worse if she had been pressing water to the golem wife's lips when those dry eyelids had snapped open.

At least in this fashion, they got it over with.

The golem wife's lips had not pulled back from her teeth like the lips of the dead were supposed to do. They opened now, just a crack.

In a voice like dried leaves rubbing together, the golem wife whispered, ". . . thirsty . . ."

Rhea's horror did not fade, but it was tempered by pity. *She's not dead, even if she's not quite alive, and she can feel thirst, and oh, god, how long as she been here?*

She tried to imagine hanging on a pole for hours—days, years— with water at her feet, unable to drink. Her mind skittered away from the image of days and years piled up like dead leaves.

Let her sleep through it. Let her not really be awake and suffering, unless someone wakes her up. Please, please, let her not be aware of it.

". . . please . . . ," whispered the dry voice.

Hurriedly, before she could change her mind, Rhea ducked down and cupped water into her hands. She lifted the makeshift cup, her fingers dripping, and set it against the cracked lips.

She had to reach up, for the pole was tall. Water poured down her wrists and soaked her shirt as the golem wife drank awkwardly over her thumb.

When the water running down her forearms had slowed to a trickle, she scooped more up, and more again. Five times Rhea gave the golem wife water to drink before she whispered, ". . . enough."

Rhea dropped her hands. She noticed suddenly that she was cold and soaked and standing in water.

". . . thank you . . ."

"I have to go back," said Rhea miserably. "I have to be back by dawn. Otherwise I'd—I'd cut you down or—oh, I don't know. Is there anything I can do?"

There was a crackling noise as the golem wife shook her head.

Rhea backed away. It seemed disrespectful to turn her back on what was, in a terrible fashion, another woman. Eventually, though, she had to look down at her feet to avoid skidding on the scum-slick stones.

When she reached the edge of the pool and looked back, the golem wife's eyes were closed and she hung limply on the pole, as unliving as a scarecrow.

Let her be asleep. Let her be mostly dead. Let her be anything but alive and awake for all this time.

Rhea turned and ran.

Chapter Fifteen

She did not run very far, because as soon as she reached the other side of the clearing, she realized that the path was gone.

Rhea staggered to a halt. It was like going down a ladder and thinking you still had another rung left beneath you, only to slam your foot into the floor.

She did not panic. It was absurd that the path was gone—it had been wide enough to accommodate a couple of horses. She was just looking in the wrong place. In her panicked flight, she'd gotten turned around.

She turned in place, looking, and there were the pool and the poles and the golem wife. But there was no path. The trees grew in a dense, unbroken wall around the edges.

Too many shocking things had happened tonight. That was undoubtedly why she was so calm. In a place where dead women were partly alive and hung on poles, getting upset about a missing path seemed futile.

"I think we have a problem," she said to the hedgehog.

The hedgehog considered this, and made put-me-down gestures with its paws. Rhea set the little creature on the ground, and it trundled up to the tree line and sat back, looking grave.

The brambles had grown in under the tree trunks, and the thickets were sewn together with vines. There were pockets where she might manage to get a few feet in, but no farther.

He made the path vanish. He made the white road appear, and now he's made the path vanish so I can't get back. He wants me to be lost out here.

And with a sudden rush of outrage, *That's not fair! He's cheating!*

She fumed for a minute while the hedgehog studied the trees. How dare Crevan cheat? Set someone an impossible task and—and—

And what?

Did you really think he'd let you go? Did you think this was something you could win?

Her thoughts stuttered to a halt.

The hedgehog was off again, trundling along the edge of the woods, snuffling in the leaves. Rhea followed, because when your future husband is a mad sorcerer, following a hedgehog sometimes seems like a good option.

It occurred to her that Lord Crevan had sent her to find the golem wife, knowing full well that she would be terrified by it.

But why? Just to scare me, like a little boy with a frog? Why would he do this to me?

And a cold voice in the back of her head whispered, *To show you the price of disobedience.*

A chill set in that had nothing to do with her wet shoes and clothes.

The hedgehog halted in front of a particular set of brambles. To Rhea, it looked the same as all the rest of the undergrowth, but the little animal snuffled at the base of the thicket, stirring up last year's leaves with its nose. Then it looked up at her, and back to the trees.

"I'd need an ax," Rhea said. A little bubble of fear rose up in her throat and burst into horrified laughter. "Oh, Lady! If I had an ax, I'd take it to him, and never mind the trees!"

I've been acting as if I could get out of this somehow—if I just said or did the right things, he'd have to let me go. But he's mad, completely mad, and he turns his wives into golems. He needs killing, not negotiation.

This thought brought her a strange sense of relief. She was not doing something wrong. She was not failing. She was not a peasant girl marrying above her station and doing it badly. She had run afoul of a murderer, that was all.

She laughed again, feeling light-headed. She had a sudden desire to grab her aunt by the wrists and shake her and yell, "See! See, I told you there was something wrong!"

The hedgehog gave her a worried look.

"Sorry," she said contritely. "I'll stop laughing. I'm not losing my mind, I promise. Losing my mind won't help, will it?"

The hedgehog managed to convey that it most definitely would *not* help.

"Right."

The hedgehog gave another pointed glance to the wall of brambles.

"Um," said Rhea. "The path is on the other side of that, isn't it?"

The hedgehog nodded.

Rhea considered for a moment, then said, "Stand back."

She lifted her boot and tried to stomp down part of the thicket. It yielded a few leaves and a calf full of thorns.

She kicked at the brambles again, and again, and then she had to stop. There was blood running down both legs, and the wall of wood and thorn had not changed in the slightest.

"I don't think it's going to happen," she told the hedgehog. It sighed.

She sat down on one of the paving stones, and the hedgehog helped her pull thorns out of her skin. They were long and jagged edged, not smooth like rose thorns. She washed her legs off in the pool and saw the blood welling up black in the moonlight.

You'd need to be wearing armor to make it through to the path. If I keep going, I won't have any skin left.

There were tears in her eyes from the pain, but she did not cry. The golem wife was too near.

I can't cry about thorns when she's been hanging from a pole for . . . however long it's been.

The hedgehog held up its paws, crossed them, and turned away.

"Errr . . ."

It turned back and held up its paws again.

"Do you want me to stay here?"

A nod.

"Okay then . . ."

It dropped back to all fours and trundled into the brambles. Thorns that would stop a human girl were no barrier to the hedgehog.

She could watch its progress for only a moment or two, and then it was gone.

I wonder if it's going for help . . .

She hoped it was. She was going to need help.

The gods help those who help themselves . . . or at least, that's what Aunt always says . . .

She circled the clearing. The sunken stones in the pool gleamed in the moonlight. The trees were black and dense and impassable.

Desperate to do *something* while she waited, she tried pulling up one of the wooden poles, hoping she could use it to beat back the thicket. It didn't even budge.

Why did he put these here? Was he planning on hanging a whole army of golem wives from them?

The mental image was so appalling that she shied away from it at once.

As the moon crawled by overhead and the hedgehog did not return, she found herself thinking, *What if it isn't coming back?*

She didn't know why it had chosen to help her in the first place. What if it had decided she was a lost cause? For all she knew, it might have gone home.

Rhea eyed the bramble wall again, considering a second attempt.

No. I can't get out like that, she decided. *If daylight comes, he'll just have to come get me, and while he's busy making marriage plans, I'll—I'll excuse myself to go to the privy and climb out the window . . . or something.*

Leaves rustled, and the hedgehog reemerged.

Rhea exhaled. "Thank goodness," she said. "I was worried—"

A second hedgehog came out of the brambles after it.

Rhea blinked. "You brought a friend . . . ?"

And then a third hedgehog emerged, and a fourth, and before she knew it, there were a dozen, and then twenty and thirty, and the whole clearing was full of tiny, fist-sized animals with prickly backs and blinking black-bead eyes.

"Oh . . . ," said Rhea, because she could think of nothing else to say.

The first hedgehog—*her* hedgehog—patted her ankle.

It turned to the others, and the lot of them crowded together, making grunting, squeaking noises, having a conversation in hedgehog tongue.

Perhaps I've lost my mind after all . . .

Then they separated. They began to waddle away and take up positions throughout the clearing. When one found its spot (Rhea could not tell what made one spot better than another, but the hedgehogs seemed to have definite opinions on the matter) it would sit down and turn its face up toward the moon.

Her hedgehog lifted its paws and squeaked.

One by one, in no pattern Rhea could determine, the other hedgehogs lifted their paws and squeaked.

Hers repeated the act. So did the others. And again. And again.

They were doing it in the same order, Rhea realized. *Look, mine starts it, then the little one on top of the rock takes up the cry, then the big one down in the hollow with the moss, then that one, then that one in the back . . .*

The hedgehogs moved faster and faster. Their squeaks dropped, becoming an odd sort of croon, as they all gazed up at the moon, lifting their paws and dropping them, over and over.

Rhea began to wonder if she was dreaming.

Something cold and slimy touched her hand. She glanced down and snatched her fingers away with a yelp, because it was a slug.

It had crawled across the paving where she was sitting and fetched up against her. When she moved out of the way, it slowly slid through the space she'd vacated, leaving a gleaming trail behind it.

Boy, did you come to the wrong place, thought Rhea, looking from the slug to the crooning hedgehogs.

Except there wasn't just one slug.

There was another one over there, and three on the paving stone next to her, and dozens coming up behind those, and—

They're summoning slugs.

The hedgehogs have called up slugs. Oh, Lady of Stones, there are thousands of them.

It was like a gardener's nightmare come to life. The slugs had fat, gleaming bodies speckled with thick gray spots. Soon the stones were crisscrossed with slime trails. As the hedgehogs kept chanting and the slugs kept emerging from the forest, the trails merged together, until it was impossible to tell where one stopped and another began.

Rhea backed up until she was nearly in the pool again, and only the mingled fear and pity she felt for the golem wife kept her from retreating clear into the water.

Gradually, the slugs converged. They wove a path between the hedgehogs and formed a blunt gray wedge as they advanced on the bramble wall.

Why would slugs come when hedgehogs call them? They're enemies.
Maybe the hedgehogs promised to stop eating them for a bit?

It made no sense to Rhea, but on the other hand, she'd just watched hedgehogs sing to the moon to summon a carpet of slugs, so clearly there was very little sense to be made of anything. She took another step back and felt water slosh against her heels.

This is unspeakably bizarre. This cannot possibly be happening. I am having a dream. Real people do not stand in ponds while hedgehogs summon an army of slugs.

She darted a glance over her shoulder and saw the golem wife hanging in the shadows.

And yet, if this is a dream, it has been going on for a very long time.

The moon was sinking now, almost behind the edge of the trees. The night was old. And the slugs had reached the brambles and were climbing into the wall of vegetation . . .

. . . and beginning to eat.

Rhea had to pick her way slowly across the slimy rocks, but even before she was halfway across the clearing, it became obvious that the slugs were devouring the thicket. They could not remove trees, but they gnawed through vines, and a dozen together could rasp away a bramble cane.

Someone who was not familiar with the havoc a slug could wreak on a vegetable garden might have been surprised by the speed at which they worked, but Rhea was not. Already she could walk a few feet into the woods—and there, very clearly, was the beginning of the orchard path.

"Thank you," breathed Rhea. "Oh, thank you! I will never step on a slug again!"

She could have sworn that the nearest slug turned its eyestalks toward her in reproach.

"Um. Sorry." It went back to eating.

Another arm's length into the woods, and another—and then there was a break in the trees, and the orchard path lay clear and visible before her.

She hurried back into the clearing, arriving in time to see her hedgehog drop its paws and stop crooning.

"Thank you," said Rhea. "Thank you all. I can't repay you, but when I've got a garden—you're all welcome, always—forever. *Thank you!*"

She snatched up her hedgehog, and it dove into her pocket. Then she turned and ran.

The way was clear. She pounded down the path, heedless of any pebbles that might turn underfoot. The overgrown orchard became more widely spaced as she went, and the brambles retreated, and the sky was gray overhead, and she was at the garden gate, and she was pounding across the cobbles, and there was Maria, standing in the doorway, and . . .

Rhea fell over the threshold and into Maria's arms, just as the sun began to rise.

Chapter Sixteen

She didn't mean to cry. She had been crying too much lately, and she didn't know Maria very well at all—she'd known her two days, really. You didn't cry in front of perfect strangers; it just wasn't done.

She assured herself of all this, then burst into tears on Maria's shoulder.

"There, there," said Maria. "It's over now, and you made it back. I'll make you some tea and some breakfast, and then you can sleep for as long as you like."

Rhea let the cook steer her to a chair and plop her down. She scrubbed at her face and took one shuddery breath, then another.

Maria set the tea in front of her, with a spoon in it to stir the honey. Rhea wrapped her cold fingers around the mug.

"She's still alive," she said out loud, and felt a sob at the bottom of her throat. "She's *alive*, Maria."

"Saw her, did you?" asked Maria grimly. "Well, and so she is."

"How—how long . . . ?"

"Long enough." The heavy lines of Maria's face were hard. "A few years."

Hot tears started up at the corner of Rhea's eyes. She could not comprehend the enormity of so much time, only that it was terrible, unthinkable. Her chest ached.

"Years! But, Maria, we, *we have to tell someone!*"

Her voice spiraled up as she spoke, and she thought, *I'm getting hysterical again,* and then she thought, *Of course I am. This is insane. Getting hysterical is absolutely sensible.*

"Sure," said Maria. "Sure." She began spooning biscuit dough onto a tray. "Who shall we tell?"

"The viscount! A priest! *Someone!*"

"His friend the viscount? A village priest who probably serves at the viscount's pleasure? Do you think they'll listen to a little girl and a fat old cook?" Maria added a bit more flour to the bowl and scraped the spoon along the side.

Her tone was absolutely reasonable, and Rhea wanted to scream. She fisted both hands in her hair. "But, but, but she's hanging there, and . . . *and you're making biscuits!*"

"Yes," said Maria. "I am. We could both sit down at the table and cry together. But in a few hours, the golem wife will still be hanging there, and there will still be no one we can tell, and the only thing that will be different is that we will be hungry. And there will be no biscuits."

Rhea slumped in the chair, trying not to sob.

Maria glanced over at her, and her face softened. "I truly don't think she suffers much," she said quietly. "He took her will, you see. She cannot even die without his permission. She likely cannot feel pain, either."

What?

On some level, Rhea knew the words were important, but they sounded meaningless in her ears.

How can someone give you permission to die? How can they stop you?

"She was thirsty," she said aloud.

"Ah," said Maria. She exhaled. "Well. That was your task, was it not? Perhaps he gave her permission to be thirsty."

There was a sound from the doorway, hardly more than a scuff of a shoe against the floor. Rhea looked up to see Ingeth.

The silent woman turned, not meeting her eyes, and walked away.

"Going to report that you came in on time, I imagine," said Maria.

"What did you mean, 'took her will'?" asked Rhea.

"Just what I said," snapped Maria. "Himself is good at taking. This one's magic, that one's will, that one's death—"

Her whole body jerked suddenly—once, twice, three times. Her arms twitched, and she staggered sideways, one hand pressed to her chest.

Rhea jumped up, sending the chair over backward.

"Maria!"

The other woman stood still for a moment, swaying in place. Then she turned and limped to a chair, setting each step as carefully as a mason laying stone.

Rhea yanked the chair out for her, and Maria fell into it. Her breath came in hard pants. "Stupid," she gasped out, one syllable to a breath, ". . . stu . . . *pid* . . ."

"What do I do?" asked Rhea, panicking. If something happened to Maria—her only human ally in this place; she could hardly count Sylvie, who was so sweetly ineffectual, and it went without saying she couldn't count Ingeth—

"Wa . . . ter . . ."

Rhea splashed water into a cup with shaking hands and held it to the cook's lips. A few swallows, and the strange fit seemed to pass. Maria put her elbows on the table and her face in her hands. Rhea hovered over her, uncertain.

"I'm fine," said Maria. "I'm an old woman who talks too much, that's all."

"But—"

Maria spread her fingers and looked at Rhea through them.

It was all the warning Rhea needed to shut her mouth.

Crevan did that. She was starting to say too much, and he did that to her. No wonder she wouldn't say anything to me earlier.

If I marry him, what will he do to me?

A hand closed over her shoulder, and she squeaked.

Ingeth jerked her head toward the doorway.

"Go on," said Maria, looking at Ingeth with hooded eyes. "I imagine my husband wants a word with you."

"So you completed my little task," said Lord Crevan.

This time he was sitting behind a desk rather than standing at the book stand. Rhea stood in front of it, feeling small and bloody and disheveled. The fact that she was standing and he was sitting should have helped, but it did not. She stared at her feet.

"You *did* complete the task, did you not?"

"I gave her something to drink," said Rhea dully.

"Good," said Crevan. "Good."

"She wasn't a scarecrow," said Rhea. A small fury roiled in her stomach. She knew that she should not speak, but she couldn't help it. Rage and terror were all bound up together, and they squeezed out words. "She was a *person*. How could you *do* that to her?"

Lord Crevan smiled. "She possessed extraordinary willpower," he said fondly. "Stubbornness, some might say, but so much more. She was quite incandescent." He flicked a hand dismissively. "It really did no good for a little baker from the capital to have a will like that, so I gave it to someone who could make better use of it."

Rhea stared at him, struck again by the feeling that she was hearing something terribly important that made no sense at all.

Her confusion must have shown on her face. Crevan stood and came toward her.

She did not want to step back, but she did anyway, hoping it looked like deference and not like terror.

Maybe it's better if he knows I'm scared of him. It's what he wants, isn't it?

Maybe I have no idea what he wants.

He stopped two paces away. "You don't understand," he said. "Well, I couldn't expect that you would."

"Um," said Rhea, because he was clearly expecting her to say something. "No. Milord."

He smiled. "Suppose you had something that you did not need, Miss Rhea."

Like a husband? she thought grimly.

"Let us say you had . . . oh . . . a bull." He steepled his fingers. "A fierce bull in a pasture. You have no cows, no other livestock, only a very fierce bull that eats your grain and breaks your fences and does you no good at all."

It occurred to Rhea that Lord Crevan had a very limited grasp of animal husbandry. There were a great many uses for a bull, not least of which were stud fees, and if the bull were truly a wretch, the butcher could make dog food and sausage out of it. Even a broken-down horse could be sold to the knackermen.

Arguing about the value of livestock with a mad sorcerer did not seem like a good idea, however, even as angry as she was.

"All right," she said. "I've got a bull."

He took another step forward. Rhea's spine bumped against the wall as she retreated.

"Now, it happens that I know someone who needs a bull very much, who will, perhaps, be in a great deal of trouble without one. They may even die without one."

Rhea had heard of people getting into a great deal of trouble with bulls—usually when crossing a pasture—but never of anyone getting into trouble *without* one. Particularly not lethal trouble.

The lord of the manor is trying to explain things to the peasant, using terms he thinks the peasant will understand. I expect I'll be even angrier

*about this presently if he doesn't turn me into a golem and hang me from
a pole.*

"I see," she said.

"So I take your bull and give it to my friend," said Lord Crevan.
"The beast is no longer eating you out of house and home, and my
friend's life is saved."

However that *works.*

"And all is for the best. You see?"

"I believe," said Rhea, "that what you are describing is called cattle
raiding. It's a hanging offense. Milord."

Lord Crevan's smile slipped slightly, and he took another half step
forward.

It occurred to Rhea that while she had every right to be furious, it
would not do her a bit of good.

*I'm being stupid. If I'm meek and agreeable, maybe I can get out of the
room, out of the house, out a window, something.*

"I would not expect a . . . country girl . . . to understand," he said.

Rhea seized the opportunity. "No, milord," she said, trying to
infuse her voice with every ounce of meekness she possessed, even
though it choked her. "I'm afraid it's quite beyond me. I know about
mills. Just . . . mills."

She stared at the floor and wished with all her heart that she were
back at the mill.

*I wouldn't care if there were a thousand gremlins and I had to pry each
one out by hand. I want to go home.*

He sighed, as if she had disappointed him. "I expect too much.
Still, you have other gifts, my dear, and you are very young . . . for now."

Something about the way he said the last words made Rhea lift her
eyes from the floor.

Not too young to marry, apparently. What does he mean?

Crevan turned away. "I shall have another little task for you this
evening," he said. "Ingeth will show you out."

Chapter Seventeen

She slept, exhausted. At a little after four in the afternoon, the house shook, and she came awake, hearing the clangor of metal and broken bells.

The floor's falling again, she thought muzzily. *The clock wife must be in a mood.*

She no longer had any problem believing that there was a clock wife. Of course there would be one.

Rhea got up. She put on the dress that she had arrived in, travel stains and all, and transferred the hedgehog between pockets. It looked up at her, eyes small and frightened.

"It will be all right," said Rhea, knowing that it was a lie. It would never be all right, not when the golem wife was hanging from her pole, not while Crevan was utterly mad and babbling about bulls and had the power of life and death and worse than death over them all.

The hedgehog gave her a look that said it knew she was lying and understood why she was doing so. It rolled into a small, prickly ball in her pocket.

She walked out of her room, her mind carefully empty. Somewhere down under her breastbone, she knew that she was leaving, this hour, this minute, come what may. So long as she did not *think* it, surely Crevan could not smell her thoughts.

The front door was unguarded. Rhea half expected to see Ingeth waiting for her, but the silent woman was nowhere to be seen.

She opened the front door and was through it before it occurred to her to worry that it might be locked.

The white road blazed before her. If it dazzled in moonlight, it blinded in daylight. Walking down it would be like walking down the blade of a polished sword.

The fountain still rang with water, presided over by the angel with sagging wings.

The hedgehog squirmed uneasily as she approached the road.

The bird golems had their heads tucked under their wings. Perhaps they were night birds and roosted by day. The same two huddled together on one side, and the third slept by itself, unmoving.

Are they going to attack me if I go under?

Rhea stepped through the arch, hands half lifted to protect her face.

The birds did not move.

Poor things. He made you like the golem wife, didn't he?

Her eyes ached from the glare, and she realized that she was holding her breath. She let it out, carefully.

Down the road. There are monsters there, I know. The hedgehog's scared of them. So am I.

I better move quickly.

She did not run. Running from the house would be like running from a dangerous animal—as if it would suddenly realize that she was prey and come after her. But she walked quickly, with her head down and her arms folded over her breast.

Dust rose up with every step, just as it had done before.

She did not look over her shoulder at the house. She wanted to believe that it was getting farther away, but she had a horrible fear that she might look back and see it right behind her.

The dust was chest high now. Sweat trickled down the back of her neck. She raised her head and saw the woods looming in front of her, a dark line crossing the white line of the road.

The road . . . moved.

At first, Rhea thought that the glare was playing tricks with her eyes. The white pavement heaved upward in a mound before subsiding. Another section bubbled up and fell away again.

Heat haze, she thought. *It must be. It must be.*

It was like no heat haze she had ever seen. The road did not shimmer, it *roiled*. It moved like a canvas with a road painted on it, billowing and subsiding as she watched.

Her footsteps slowed, then stopped entirely as the road continued to boil in front of her. "What's going on?" she said aloud.

The hedgehog made a small sound of distress. Rhea leapt sideways as the pavers started to heave under her feet. The dust rose up like steam.

She landed badly, almost turning her ankle, and stumbled away. The hedgehog shrieked. She ran for the grass on the side of the road, but it seemed to be miles away, as if the road had grown, and there were bubbles heaving up between her and it.

Roads don't boil. This isn't happening. It's a trick to keep you from leaving, that's all.

If it was a trick, it was a very effective one.

She staggered backward. Back was the only way that was even remotely clear.

No! Not back, not toward the house! The trees—if I could just reach the trees!

The dust roiled up, higher than a man now, forming a wall between Rhea and the trees. There were faces in it now, faces with yawning mouths and teeth like pine needles, faces that had never been human, faces that were not quite human enough.

They looked down at her, and Rhea knew that these *things* on the white road could see her.

Her arms hung slack at her sides. She could feel the road moving beneath her feet, and yet she could not force herself to run toward the trees.

They're only dust. They can't actually hurt me. Surely *they can't actually hurt me.*

The dust faces moved closer. They were solidifying as they approached, the air becoming thick as gauze. Creatures plucked whole from childhood nightmares wriggled and squirmed in the air and became the nightmares of a hardened adult.

And still Rhea could not move.

The hedgehog shrieked in her pocket, a shriek like that of a rat in a trap. It broke the spell.

Rhea turned and ran.

The road rippled underneath her. If she stumbled, she knew she would die. The things on the road would tear her apart, out of hunger, out of hatred, out of some alien emotion that she did not understand.

She was running back to the house of her enemy, but she did not care.

Her feet pounded on the road. Her steps raised no dust now, she saw—perhaps it had all gone to give shape to the bodies of the things behind her.

There was no sound at all except for the slap of her shoes on the road and her hoarse breathing and the whimpering of the hedgehog.

She could see faces in her peripheral vision, long grasping hands (if they were hands). She did not dare look at them. She had to look at the next step and the next one and trust her feet because her feet were the only things that could save her.

She dove beneath the arch and into the courtyard, remembering to fall sideways to shield the hedgehog. The shoulder of her dress shredded, and the flesh underneath raked across the cobbles.

She lay there, her breath hurling itself in and out of her chest, waiting for a dusty claw to reach out under the arch and drag her back to the road.

It did not come.

After a while, she sat up. The hedgehog shuddered in her pocket. She looked through the arch.

The road lay straight and quiet. The dust danced as if it had been caught in a stray breath of wind.

Her entire escape attempt had lasted less than ten minutes.

And then, because she could think of nothing else to do, Rhea went into the house and returned to her room. She pulled the covers over her head and curled into a very small ball, as if she were a hedgehog herself.

Chapter Eighteen

Rhea woke as the sun was setting. The covers were still pulled over her head.

It always works with monsters. They can't get you under the blankets.

But those were childhood fancies, and she was in a house surrounded by real monsters and locked inside with a grown-up one who walked about in a human skin. Leaving the house was clearly not an option.

What were those things?

She grimaced. *Never mind. They're . . . out there. I'm in here.*

Crevan's in here, too.

If she refused to get out of bed, he would undoubtedly count that as a task failed, and then . . .

. . . then, Miss Rhea, I'll marry you.

She grimaced again and swung her feet out onto the floor.

Not that it matters. He's probably going to keep setting me tasks until I fail at one.

Why doesn't he just marry me outright? Does he like to play with his prey before he eats it, like a cat?

She put the hedgehog in her pocket and went down to the kitchen.

"Not up for cooking tonight, child," said Maria hoarsely. The cook was sitting at the far end of the table, looking weary. "There's bread and cheese and raisins on the table for you, and you can wrap up a bit to take with you tonight."

Rhea looked up, startled.

"There's a note," Maria said, nodding to it. "Can you read?"

"I can," said Rhea. "I'm better with figures." She picked up the note.

Tonight you must go to the grave of Lady Elegans and place flowers on it.

Leave at moonrise and return before the sun.

This is a small task, Miss Rhea, but should you prove unwilling or unable to complete it, I will marry you.

Crevan

Rhea folded it and set it back down on the table. She did not want to put it in her pocket. Lord Crevan had touched it. She rubbed her hands on the side of her skirt before picking up the bread knife.

At least I don't have to talk to him. Does he know I was on the white road? Did he laugh at me for running from the monsters? Was he pleased that I was scared?

"Lady Elegans isn't so bad," said Maria, breaking into her thoughts. "She was a proud woman, but not a cruel one."

"Is she really dead?" asked Rhea skeptically.

"Oh, yes. Dead and in the ground and not coming back. When your life goes elsewhere, that's the end of the matter. It's not like misplacing your *death*."

"Okay . . . ," said Rhea, though she truly didn't understand the difference.

She set the hedgehog on the table. It began shoveling raisins into its mouth, with every evidence of enjoyment.

I wish I were as resilient as a hedgehog.

"The white road—" she began.

"Is dangerous," said Maria flatly.

This is not a safe topic of conversation, then. Damnation.

She would have liked to ask about the beasts on the road. She would have liked to ask—well, in truth, there were a few thousand questions that Rhea would have liked to ask, and she didn't know that she was going to get the chance. What would set Crevan off? Maria looked worn out. Would another bolt of . . . whatever that was . . . kill her? Would Crevan risk killing off his cook?

He can probably just marry a new one.

She applied herself to the bread and cheese.

After a few minutes, she said, "How do I get to the graveyard?"

"Out the garden gate," said Maria, "and turn to your right. There's a little road, or there will be when you go. It's a country graveyard, and not a bad place."

"It'll be harder coming back," said Rhea, staring at the cheese. "The hedgehogs helped me last time."

Maria nodded. "I felt magic," she said. "A little wildwood magic." She offered the hedgehog another raisin, which was graciously accepted. "It was kind, and there's little enough kindness around here. I shouldn't expect it a second time, if I were you."

Rhea's heart sank. On some level, she had been counting on the hedgehog to come through for her again.

The little animal gave her an apologetic look and patted her wrist with its paw.

"Not your fault," said Rhea. "You helped me once. I suppose this time I'm on my own."

"I shouldn't say that," said Maria. "Our thoughts go with you. For some of us, that's worth more than others." She slid a knife across the table. "It's nearly moonrise. Go cut some flowers for the grave."

It was not a terribly good bouquet—a few purple asters and some sweet-smelling herbs. Still, the note hadn't specified that she bring white lilies or anything, and it wasn't as if she had much choice.

She put the knife in the pocket that didn't contain a hedgehog and set off down the graveyard path.

This one turned to neither brambles and thickets nor white dust, but wound around the edge of the great manor house and into the weedy ruins of a former lawn. Foxtail grass and weeds rose waist-high in places, but the path was shorn to an inch. It was springy underfoot. A small covey of quail picked its way across the path in front of Rhea, and she paused to let it pass.

I don't have a great deal of time, but I think being polite to animals is probably a very good idea . . .

The hedgehog was warm in her pocket. There had barely been time for her to consider the little creature's magic, but now, walking briskly down the path, she found her mind returning to it.

A little wildwood magic . . . the hedgehog said it wasn't enchanted when I asked. I wonder if they can all do that, if you get enough of them together . . .

She'd never heard of such a thing, but the world was a strange place. If there were humans with odd little magical talents, perhaps there were hedgehogs with them, too. Maybe she just happened to have a slug speaker in her pocket.

"If I survive this," she said to the hedgehog, out loud, "we're going to have a very long talk."

It poked its snout out of her pocket and gave her a dubious look.

"I'll talk," she clarified. "You can . . . um . . . mime. We'll play charades?"

It occurred to her, yet again, that the possibility she was going mad would explain a great many things.

Still, not much that I can do about it if I am. I suppose if you're mad, you just carry on doing whatever seems best. Maybe the wheelwright's son had a very good reason for putting trousers on that pig. Maybe if you've spent a week in a fairy mound, it is incredibly obvious that all pigs need trousers.

Maybe I'm overthinking this.

The fields around her changed. The grass grew taller, until she suspected it was no longer an overgrown lawn but an old hayfield. It was taller than her head in places, so that she walked through a rustling tunnel that glowed silver in the moonlight.

When the wind blew, the grass bent and the tunnel seemed to lean sideways, murmuring in a hundred restless voices.

It was not an unpleasant place. Rhea would have rather liked it, if she had been back in the village. She had always been fond of grain fields—it was part of being a miller's daughter, knowing that all the wheat rippling around you would eventually wind up at the mill. There was a proprietary quality to her enjoyment.

This was not quite a grain field. There were too many weeds of the prickly, thorny, bristly variety, and it would have been a rather unpleasant lot to bring down to the threshing floor. But the grasses bent properly in the wind and made familiar rustling sounds when they did, and Rhea's heart seized with homesickness, even as she was comforted by it.

If I have to marry him, he can't keep me in the house all the time. I could walk here. This is not a bad place.

When she found the graveyard, it was not at the end of the path, but more or less in the middle of it. The path split in two and went in a broad circle. In the center, a low wrought-iron fence with broken finials enclosed a small country graveyard.

It was not the sort of place Rhea where would have expected to find the grave of a great lady. (Maria had called her Lady Elegans, so surely she was noble?) It was a little clutter of gravestones, softened by moss, like the family graveyards found on old farms.

The gate stood open, and even if it had not, she could have easily stepped over it. A hare moved away as she approached, not in a run, just a few unconcerned hops.

It was all very peaceful. Rhea had a hard time believing that it stood so close to Lord Crevan's home. It seemed like she should be able to feel his malice, even here, but there was not even a whisper of him.

There were only a dozen graves. Rhea walked between them, looking for names, and found Elegans written on most of them.

Is this their graveyard? Did this used to be their manor house, and Crevan married into it? Or is the world just twisted around again and I've come to their graveyard by magic?

"And which is Lady Elegans?" she asked aloud. "Is this part of the test? Find the correct grave?"

A dozen graves. Eight of them had the name Elegans.

Rhea felt a bubble of panic. *No one told me her first name. What if I put the flowers on the wrong grave? I'll fail the task.*

She looked down at the gravestones again . . . and then blew her breath out, hard.

Don't be ridiculous. This is not hard. Aunt would figure it out in a trice. It's no worse than when we get grain from the Smiths.

There were six Smith families in town, all of whom were descended from the same patriarch and all of whom hated one another passionately, egged on by that selfsame patriarch. Working out which Smith household was due which bags of grain could be an exciting prospect if the notes were not exact.

This would be easier if there were dates on the stones. I could work backward from there . . .

But there were no dates. There were a few phrases chiseled here and there, and several carvings, but no dates. Time had apparently stopped in this place.

Of the eight gravestones, three had male names. It was unlikely that Lady Elegans had been named John or Jack—though not impossible, Rhea had to admit, as the mayor two towns over had been born with the name Jack and was the most elegantly dressed woman in three counties. But both of those stones had badly worn lettering, as if they were very old, and the third male headstone was very small and inscribed with the words "Beloved Son."

There were five headstones, each with a woman's name or no name at all, and two of those were also weathered. The one next to "Beloved Son" said "Beloved Daughter" and was no larger than its counterpart.

Children, most likely, thought Rhea, *carried off in a plague. Poor things.*

That left her with two gravestones.

One had sharp, clearly edged writing. "Sophia Elegans." The other was a trifle more worn, but the stone looked softer, and it read "Catherine Elegans."

Sophia Elegans's stone was decorated with a carving of ivy around the edges, and underneath it said "Beloved Wife."

Catherine Elegans had a carving of an angel and the words "The World Is Greater For Your Gift."

Rhea considered this.

It was hard to imagine Lord Crevan writing "Beloved Wife" under something and meaning it, although it was perfectly plausible that he had waved a hand to someone—probably Ingeth, or perhaps her predecessor—and said, "Have it say something appropriate, 'beloved wife' or some such," and thought no more about it.

On the other hand, there had been that long and rather opaque discussion about gifts. And bulls. Rhea scowled.

She glanced at the sky. The moon was high overhead, not yet beginning its downward slide.

And as soon as I'm done here, the path is going to close up or some such nonsense, and it will take half the night to get away from it.

She could afford to be both annoyed and terrified by this—rather than merely terrified—because she was very nearly sure that Lord Crevan would not kill her *before* he married her. For whatever perverse reason, he seemed very interested in marriage.

Afterward, of course, is another matter. I suppose he killed Lady Elegans, whether she was Sophia or Catherine.

After the golem wife, the prospect of being merely murdered seemed almost unremarkable.

I suppose I shan't enjoy it very much if he does it to me. Then again, I suppose no one ever really enjoys dying, however it happens.

Well, enough of this.

She pulled the bouquet from her pocket and divided it in two. Each had a few stems of asters and a sprig of rosemary.

She laid one on the grave of Sophia Elegans, Beloved Wife, and one on the grave of Catherine Elegans, The World Is Greater For Your Gift, and stepped back.

"I don't know if I'm supposed to say something," she announced to the graves. "My name's Rhea. I'm the miller's daughter. I suppose I'm going to be Lord Crevan's wife, if I can't get out of it. I guess that makes us . . . errr . . . something? Not sisters. Something else. Anyway. The flowers are for you. I hope wherever you are, you're . . . um . . . well?"

It was not the most graceful speech ever made in a graveyard. Rhea felt vaguely absurd, and her face grew hot, even though no one had heard her but the hedgehog and the dead.

She turned away.

A dog stood outside the iron fence, staring at her.

Chapter Nineteen

Here we are, then, thought Rhea grimly.

It was not a nice-looking dog. It had a short coat and the cool, professional look of a sheep killer.

Rhea measured the distance to the open gate. The dog was on the opposite side of the graveyard from it, and while she could not hope to outrun the animal for more than a few paces, she needed only get to the gate and haul it shut. It opened out, with a heavy metal cuff that slammed down over the bar, so once she shut it, the dog would not be able to pull it open.

And then it will jump over this ridiculous three-foot fence and tear my throat out. Even if it doesn't, I'll be stuck in the graveyard.

"Nice dog?" said Rhea.

The dog stared at her. The moon burned green in its eyes.

"*Good* dog," said Rhea, and then she turned and bolted for the gate.

The dog took off silently, which was a bad sign. If it had barked at least, perhaps it would have been a sign that the dog was as nervous as she was. But it did not bark. It merely ran.

As she reached the gate, a second dog slipped out of the tall grass and charged her.

The hinges made a shattering squeal when she yanked on them, and there was a bad moment when it looked as if the gate was not going to close at all.

"Oh, no," Rhea said, and threw herself backward, hauling on the gate with all her might.

The resistance gave so suddenly that she fell over backward, and the gate struck the gatepost and bounced open again.

The second dog could not slow down in time. It rammed its shoulder into the gate, forcing it up against the gatepost, and Rhea scrambled to her knees in time to jam the metal cuff down, locking it in place.

The first dog arrived and joined the second. It jammed its muzzle through the bars, and Rhea retreated.

"I like dogs," said Rhea weakly as the dogs snarled at her through the gate. "I'm not scared of them at all. Really."

The first dog's throat worked, and a sound like black, snarling laughter came out of its snout.

That is not a dog noise.

Even the viscount's hounds, when they went after foxes, did not make noises like that.

The second dog giggled at her. It *giggled!*

Rhea took a couple of steps back from the fence.

"You're not dogs," she said.

Something laughed behind her, and she turned to see a third dog monster, its paws resting on the fence.

They could jump it. They could jump it easy. *I could* step *over this damn fence.*

But they did not. They snarled and snickered at her, pacing around the edges of the fence, and they set their broad paws up on the crosspieces of the fence. She did not want to look too closely at their paws. They were long and equipped with something that resembled fingers.

Rhea stood in the middle of the graveyard, atop the grave of Sophia Elegans, Beloved Wife . . . and found that she was *furious.*

It was so *stupid*! The dog monsters were so obviously there to frighten her into staying in the graveyard. They could have killed her in a heartbeat, but instead they were holding her prisoner, pacing the edges of the fence, making those nasty undoglike noises.

"He's cheating," said Rhea savagely. "This is just like the brambles last night. He wants to make sure I don't get home."

He was worse than a swan. At least swans made no pretenses. They just went for you; they didn't set you up to fail.

She shoved her hands in her pockets. The hedgehog prickled against her fingers.

"Do you want me to put you down?" she asked. "I'm about to do something very stupid."

The hedgehog turned a bright eye up toward her and shrugged, as if to indicate that perhaps it was the time for very stupid acts.

Rhea stalked toward the gate.

The first two dog monsters were bunched up there—*First and Second,* she named them in her head, *and the other one is Third.* Not very good names, but she didn't have time to be clever.

First jammed his head through the bars again, lips writhing against his teeth.

Rhea yanked the kitchen knife out of her pocket and stabbed the dog monster in the face.

It was not a terribly good stab. Millers' daughters do not traditionally spend a great deal of time engaged in single combat. She stabbed straight down, and the blade skidded across the monster's muzzle and over its tender nose.

First shrieked, a sound somewhere between a yelp and a scream of pain, and yanked its head out of the gate. The knife went flying.

It took far too long to find the blade again, even with the moon winking off the steel. But the dog monsters were not attacking her, as she'd half expected. First had his head down, pawing at his face like a dog that has been stung by a bee, and Second had retreated away from the fence.

Rhea held the knife up in front of her. Her hands were shaking. She shot a glance over her shoulder. Third was watching her silently, but it had not jumped over the fence.

"Well?" she shouted. Her voice trembled horribly, but she didn't care. The important thing was to say the words. "Well? Come on, then! Are you going to do anything?"

Second bared his teeth at her, but did not move.

She clutched the knife in front of her. The silver ring on her finger seemed unnaturally large, so large it almost got in the way of the hilt, but surely that was impossible.

If I stop to think about this, I'll lose my nerve. They're not supposed to kill me. Whatever Crevan wants me for—and he wants something, clearly, with all this talk of gifts—he'll need me alive to marry me.

I think.

Well, the golem wife wasn't alive, but . . . well, she's . . . oh, hell, who knows when he did that to her?

Quickly, before she could think herself out of it, she unlocked the gate and pushed it open.

Second charged at her. Rhea swept the knife in front of her and shouted, "Try it! Go ahead!"

Adrenaline made bright sparks in her vision—but Second stopped. The dog monster halted, bouncing on stiff legs. The air filled with growls.

She inched her way sideways, keeping her back to the fence. From the corner of her eye, she saw Third slink around the bottom of the graveyard, coming toward her.

"I see you," she said. "Don't think I don't." The dog monster stopped in its tracks.

Second rushed forward suddenly, taking advantage of her distraction, and grabbed a mouthful of her skirts.

Compared to a swan's neck, the dog monster was an absurdly large target. Rhea kicked up hard and caught Second's throat with her boot. He let out a gagging cough and fell back.

She spun in time to brandish the knife at Third, who immediately retreated.

Rhea's breath came in short pants, and sweat streamed down her back and between her breasts. *Much more of this and I'm going to pass out from sheer panic . . .*

First's head was up now. There was black blood on his muzzle and a murderous look in his eye.

It occurred to Rhea that while Lord Crevan might have instructed— or enchanted, or whatever—the dog monsters not to kill her, *Lord Crevan wasn't here.* And she had made this one extremely angry.

First lunged.

Rhea sank down into a crouch and lifted the knife, prepared to sell her life as dearly as she could.

Something slammed into the dog monster from the side, a great dark shape that picked it up and threw it aside. First flew a dozen feet through the air and landed impossibly hard. It sounded like a sack of wet laundry being dropped onto stone.

Second spun away from Rhea and leapt for the intruder. The dark shape jerked its head sideways, and Second screamed in sudden pain and fell back, limping.

The moonlight streamed down on a broad, hairy back and heavy teeth.

It's a bear.

It was gigantic. It looked like a cow or a pony. Shaggy rolls of fat hung over its sides, and its paws were the size of platters. This was a bear fattened up on autumn, ready for a long winter's sleep.

The bear looked at her with tiny glittering eyes, and Rhea looked back. She was still holding the knife, which now seemed about as useful as a toothpick.

"Nice bear . . . ?" said Rhea hopelessly.

She knew *of* bears, of course. She'd heard stories. Bears were creatures that lived out in the woods somewhere, like wolves and bandits and wisent, and the only humans who interacted with them were hunters and the characters in the more unfortunate sort of fairy tale.

Now and again a bear would take a pig that had been turned out to fatten up on acorns, but that was as much interaction as anyone in the village regularly had with bears. Rhea had never actually seen one, only pictures in books.

She'd known they were large, but the pictures she'd seen made them look like thick-bodied, tailless wolves, not like hairy mountains.

Her only vaguely coherent thought was that if she survived, she was going to demand better illustrations.

The bear moved.

She did not try to dodge. It moved faster than anything that big had a right to move. By the time she realized that it was running directly *at* her, dodging would have been laughable.

She closed her eyes.

Fur brushed against her left arm. The fence at her back shuddered. Something yelped.

Rhea opened her eyes again—*Closing my eyes was stupid*—and had time to see Third go flying past her at eye level. It struck the ground not far from First and did not move again.

The bear turned its head and growled.

It was too much for Second. The injured dog monster fled, limping, and left its dead comrades behind.

Rhea stood very still.

Perhaps if I don't move, it won't notice I'm here?

She turned her head, very slowly, and saw the bear looming about five feet away from her. It was so close that she could feel the heat radiating off its body.

As she watched, the bear sat up and went, "Whuff!"

It was looking directly at her.

Well, so much for that idea.

Rhea took a deep breath, let it out, and said, "Errr . . . thank you, bear?"

The bear whuffed again. It sounded almost like laughter. The way it was sitting up, the breadth of its shoulders, made her think of someone . . . and surely that was crazy. It couldn't be, although in a world where hedgehogs sang up slug armies and men made golems of their wives and the floor fell away at midnight . . .

"Maria?" said Rhea doubtfully.

The bear shook its head, then dropped to all fours and bumped its muzzle against Rhea's shoulder, like a good-natured dog. Rhea staggered a bit and braced herself against the iron fence.

Well, if it isn't *Maria . . .*

(Rhea was just fine with it *not* being Maria, mind you, because a werebear in the house would have been rather difficult to wrap her mind around—and anyway, if she was a werebear, why hadn't she just eaten Crevan? It would have solved a lot of problems for all of them. Still . . .)

"Maria said she had a familiar once," said Rhea slowly. "A she-bear the size of a cow. Is *that* who you are?"

The bear let out another "Whuff!" and rubbed her muzzle on Rhea's arm. Rhea had to cling to the iron crosspiece to avoid being lifted clean off her feet.

"Oh . . . ," she said faintly. "It's . . . um . . . lovely to meet you . . ."

An irritated clicking came from her skirt pocket. The hedgehog poked its nose over the edge and gave the bear a very stern look.

"Whuff?"

"Chik-ik-ik!"

The bear looked abashed and retreated several feet away. Rhea brushed herself off.

Huffing in annoyance, the hedgehog settled back into its pocket. Rhea could feel it stomping around, and gritted her teeth against the prickling.

"So," said Rhea. "Um. I'm going now. I suppose you . . . errr . . . would you like to come with me?"

She was torn between hoping very much that the bear would come with her—what if there were more dog monsters?—and hoping that the bear would amble off and leave her alone. It seemed friendly, but having an animal that size *right there* was unsettling.

The bear strode out alongside her. Rhea decided to be grateful.

It had occurred to her that the road she was on continued past the graveyard. Where did it go?

Could this be a road out? Will he send more dog things to stop me?

Well, she had a bear beside her. She was likely as safe from monsters as she would ever be.

Rhea took a dozen steps past the graveyard. The path ran upward here, over the crest of a low hill.

What's on the other side? What if I can escape? I won't know where I am, but if the bear can come and go without Crevan knowing, maybe I can follow . . .

She set out briskly.

Under the moon, the grass resembled a silver sea. Night birds called to each other, and she heard a frog ratcheting to itself from the woods.

It was peaceful again.

They walked. The bear took one step for every three of Rhea's.

They reached the top of the hill.

Rhea looked down and let out a long sigh.

The white road blazed in the moonlight.

It lay like a bar across the path, like a wall made of dust and light and unknown magic.

The bear gave a startled whuff and sat back on her haunches. In Rhea's pocket, the hedgehog wiggled in alarm.

"It's all right," said Rhea, feeling light-headed. "It's all right. We'll go back to the house. I only wanted to see."

She backed up, watching the road as if it were a snake. She did not want to turn her back on it.

The bear followed her, making deep grumbling noises in her chest.

They turned back toward the manor house, and the silver field.

The grass rippled as something approached. Rhea tensed as she watched the wave approach them, and the bear halted and stood up on her hind legs.

The wave stopped, then reversed itself very quickly.

Once it was gone, Maria's familiar dropped back to all fours, grumbling.

"What was that?" asked Rhea, forgetting momentarily that no one could answer her.

The bear glanced at her. After a moment, the beast wrinkled up her muzzle and bared her teeth, then shrugged.

"Ah," said Rhea. "Not friendly."

The bear grunted.

They encountered no more trouble along the way. Once or twice something looked out from the grass—Rhea caught a glimpse of flat green eyes reflecting moonlight—but nothing stepped onto the path.

When the manor house loomed in the distance, the bear stopped. She stood up again, gazing at the house as if it were an enemy.

"I know," said Rhea glumly. "But I have to go back. I don't know how to get home from here, and even if I did, he could find my parents."

The bear sighed and rested her muzzle across Rhea's shoulder. Rhea had to lock her knees to support the weight.

The bear was hot and smelled of beast. She sighed again, and her breath steamed over Rhea's cheek. It smelled rank and damp and gloriously alive all at once.

Then the bear pulled away and ambled into the grass, leaving behind a trail of broken stems—a dark swath that resisted the rippling moonlight.

Rhea watched her go for only a moment. There were still things in the grass after all, and her protector was leaving. She hurried down the path to the house.

Nothing accosted her on the lawn. She glanced up the side of the house, at the windows that looked down at her like eyes, and it occurred to her that while there were a great many windows on the outside, there weren't enough rooms to account for them on the inside. Lord Crevan's study had a few, and there was a narrow little slot in her bedroom, like an arrow slit in a castle wall.

Even if you counted all the narrow bedrooms in a row, they wouldn't add up to this many windows, nor did she remember them being so large and hollow-looking.

Hmm.

She shook her head. *I don't know why I'm surprised. Of all the terrible things in that house, the lack of adequate windows inside should be pretty far down the list. For all I know, there's a space between the interior walls and the outside windows, and he's crammed it full of wives.*

She immediately wished she hadn't thought of that. She snuck a glance at the window nearest her, half afraid there would be faces pressed against the glass.

There was only a reflection of the sky and the lawn. Rhea breathed a sigh of relief.

Things are bad enough here without me inventing new ways to scare myself.

She stepped into the kitchen. Maria was seated at the table and looked up at her with a faint, secret smile. "You made it back, child. Good."

"Do you ever sleep?" asked Rhea.

"All the time," said Maria. "But mostly here at the table."

"Isn't that uncomfortable?"

"Plenty of time to lie down in the grave." Maria stretched her arms out. "I suppose you'll want some tea—"

A shadow fell over the doorway.

Rhea saw Maria's eyes widen, and she turned.

It was Lord Crevan.

She expected him to say something to her—something about the task or her completion of it—but instead he leveled his gaze at Maria.

"There was magic afoot just now," he said coldly.

"Aye, there was," said Maria. "And that means it wasn't mine, my lord husband, because you know as well as I do that I've not got a drop left in me."

Ah, thought Rhea. She'd suspected, of course, that Maria wasn't a witch any longer, but she hadn't known for sure.

"Then whose?" snapped Crevan, his voice like a lash. "Don't lie to me."

"I don't know," said Maria. "That's the truth, if you'd like it."

Crevan's nostrils were pinched. It dawned on Rhea that he was angry, really angry, and that frightened her. She did not like him cold and sly and amused, but it seemed preferable to—or at least less danger-ous than—this sudden white rage.

He swung around to face Rhea, and she shrank back, grateful the table was between them, wishing the bear were there, too.

"You're no witch," he said. "It wasn't you. But last night and tonight, you had aid. What was it?"

Rhea shoved her hands in her skirt pocket and cupped a hand over the hedgehog, heedless of the prickles.

"Tell me!" he snapped, taking a step toward her.

"There was a bear," said Rhea hurriedly, afraid that if he came too close, he'd smell whatever magic clung to the hedgehog. The bear was well away, and probably well able to defend herself. The hedgehog was no match for a boot, let alone an enraged sorcerer.

Maria laughed. "Still out there, is she?"

Crevan spun around to look at her. Rhea felt as if she'd been standing too close to the fire and had been allowed to step away just before the sparks caught her dress on fire.

"Your doing, wife?" he said.

"You know it wasn't. I couldn't call her now if I tried." Maria shrugged her vast shoulders. "She does what she wants. Perhaps it amused her to help this girl."

"I should have killed that beast years ago," muttered Crevan.

Maria shrugged again.

Crevan ran a hand through his hair. "Very well." He laughed suddenly. "Very well. I shall consider this. You've done the task for tonight, I assume?"

"I laid flowers on the grave," said Rhea.

He nodded. "Good. Good. Come to my study after dinner. I'll have another task for you."

"Of course you will," muttered Rhea, but she waited until after he had left to say it.

Maria exhaled and went for tea. Rhea stifled a sigh. Her mother also believed that tea was the cure for all problems—or at least, that most problems would not get any worse in the time it took to boil water, and you'd feel a little better off with a cup of tea in you.

"Was that your familiar?" she asked as Maria swung the kettle off the stove.

Maria grinned, fierce and sudden. "Can't swear to it," she said. "But if there's another bear in these woods that's well inclined toward young women, I'm sure I don't know who it could be."

She poured water into the teapot, whistling tunelessly to herself. Rhea propped her chin up in her hand and watched.

"Mind you," said Maria as she set the tea to steep, "I'm not surprised. This house touches more forests than one. And she was always a devil for finding her way. I only hope she can find her way out again."

"What do you mean, 'more forests'?" asked Rhea.

Apparently this was not a dangerous question, because Maria answered easily, without a glance at the ceiling. "A great many of them, I should think. Your village and mine. Sylvie's, Ingeth's . . . I don't know for certain, but I expect we're also next to a patch of woods close to the city, if only so the groceries can get delivered." She shook her head. "It's a great magic."

Rhea nodded. She'd suspected for some time that there was something strange about the manor's location. You couldn't hide a house this size within walking distance of a village, let alone multiple villages. "Did . . . uh . . . Himself do it?"

Now Maria did pause. Her next words had a carefully chosen quality to them, like a woman picking her way across treacherous ground. "He's very powerful," she said. "Certainly he is the master of this house."

She caught Rhea's eye and shook her head. *No.*

This gave Rhea something to think about while she finished her tea.

Did she mean that the house was like this before? Did someone make the house this way?

If it touches many forests, does that give me a better chance of running away? It was clear that Crevan controlled the paths in and out of the orchard, if the dogs and the sudden growth of brambles were any indication. And the path had gone straight to the white road after the graveyard. But that didn't mean that he could watch *all* the paths.

If I find a different path, will I wind up somewhere a thousand miles from the mill? I could wind up halfway to the capital city, and he could be dragging my parents out of bed and setting the mill on fire. Great. And besides, even if he didn't create the magic, he clearly knows how to use it.

She turned the hedgehog loose in the garden and went up to bed in a pensive state of mind.

Chapter Twenty

She woke in the afternoon when the floor fell. This time, she did not go back to sleep. The clothes she wore were getting stiff with dirt, but she was no more eager to replace them now than she had been before. Perhaps she could do some washing up.

Maria nodded to her when she came down, and nodded again once she made her request. "Certainly. There's a laundry. It's big enough for a dozen. You won't have any problems."

Clad in borrowed clothing—Sylvie's, Rhea suspected, as the cuffs of the pants fell halfway up her shins—she went to work pounding the dirt out of her clothes.

The laundry was a cavernous room. "Big enough for a dozen" didn't do it justice, unless you meant a dozen elephants. The tiles were cool underfoot, and the ceiling was so high it was lost to dimness.

Why is it so large? Does it date back to when the manor house was built?

Even the smallest tub could have held an entire family's worth of clothes. She ran a few inches of hot water into it and set to work.

Scrubbing the clothes left her hands busy but her mind free to wander. If it wandered too far, Rhea would begin to think familiar—and utterly useless—thoughts about how completely mad it was that there was a murderer in the house and she was doing laundry.

Well, as Maria would say, if I sit down and cry, nothing will change and I still won't have clean laundry.

She would not think of the night's task. That way lay only dread.

She thought instead of the house itself, so large and so empty. With the ballroom and the long dining hall, it was a house meant for entertaining. It was obviously made for dozens of people and hundreds of servants, not for one man and a half-dozen wives.

I imagine I'm staying in the servants' quarters.

There was another wing off the opposite side of the hall—Maria had gestured toward it earlier when she mentioned Sylvie, so presumably the blind woman slept in a room over there. And Ingeth had to sleep somewhere, too.

Which meant more bedrooms, and . . . oh, sitting rooms, probably, and parlors, and whatever extra rooms nobles needed to keep their nobility in. The house went on and on, and there was the matter of all those large windows she had seen from the outside, which must go to other rooms that she had not yet seen.

Perhaps when I'm a wife, instead of a fiancée, I'll get a bigger bedroom.

Rhea made a painful sound, halfway between a laugh and a cough, at that thought.

Crevan obviously hadn't built the house, even if his ultimate plan was to marry a hundred wives and make space for them all.

Everything I've seen him make has been sort of awful. All those golems . . . if he tried to build a house, it would probably be a golem house.

Rhea scowled. That was not a pleasant thought. Walls of dried skin and the roof lashed on with black leather thongs . . . no, not a pleasant thought at all.

Still, if he didn't create the magic, it must be attached to the house somehow. Maria said the house touches many forests. Perhaps magic runs in the family, and one of his ancestors built the place.

Yes, it would make sense if it were a family seat. He's a noble, and they inherit buildings more often than they create them. I suppose it's probably been in the family for hundreds of years. Someone's family, anyway.

Presumably he'll pass it on to his heirs . . . not that he has *any heirs . . .*

Her hands slowed. She turned the little cake of soap over in her fingers, not seeing it.

. . . yet.

A slow wash of adrenaline went through her body, leaving her cold. Her fingers shook despite the heat from the water.

Is that what he wants from me? Children?

She stared into the tub without seeing it. Suds drifted over the surface.

I can't have children. I'm fifteen. I mean, I could, but—that's a stupid thing to want from me. You're not supposed to have babies for at least a couple more years. Everybody knows that really young mothers die more often. I don't even bleed regularly yet.

The midwives would howl.

She wondered if she'd even be allowed a midwife, or if it would be Maria and her endless cups of tea.

Or Ingeth.

Oh, dear Lady of Stones. I will kill myself first. I really, truly will. It shouldn't be hard around here. I'll go get a midnight snack and fall through the floor. I would rather plummet to my death than try to have a baby with Ingeth poking around down there.

I think I actually mean that.

She pressed her forearm against her face, tilting her hands so the soap wouldn't run into her eyes. Her head ached at the mere thought.

No. No, that would be stupid. He's not stupid. Completely mad and obviously evil, but not stupid. If he wanted an heir, he'd probably marry someone who has proved she can have children. Some attractive young widow with big hips or something.

Rhea grabbed her laundry out of the tub and hauled the dripping weight over to the drying racks.

If not children, though . . .

He takes something from every one of his wives. I don't know how, and I don't always know what. He took Maria's magic and Sylvie's sight and Ingeth's voice and maybe he killed Lady Elegans by taking her life—and Maria said something about the golem wife's will, although I don't quite understand how that would work . . .

What is he going to take from me?

It occurred to Rhea later that evening that she could simply *ask*. For all she knew, he might tell her.

She did not get a chance. When she presented herself in front of Crevan's study, Ingeth was waiting. The silent woman glowered at her.

"Did he take away your voice?" asked Rhea conversationally.

Ingeth's breath hissed inward, and she wheeled around, one hand raised. Rhea jumped back to avoid the blow.

For a moment, she thought the other woman might actually block her from entering the study. But Ingeth only stared at her, her chest heaving, and then turned back and struck the door with her open hand.

"Enter," called Crevan.

Do I apologize? I didn't realize—or I suppose I did, but I didn't think she'd—oh, damn . . .

Ingeth turned her back, the lines of her shoulders as straight as if they had been made with a ruler.

Rhea gritted her teeth. She didn't like Ingeth, and yes, she'd wanted to needle her a little, but there was a difference between needling someone and punching them in the gut.

"Sorry," she muttered. The line of Ingeth's back didn't soften.

She entered the study, her stomach roiling. Was she going to get light, amused, sardonic Crevan, or enraged Crevan?

I suppose it doesn't matter. They're all different shades of the same madman.

He was at the book stand again. The last light through the window tinted the book and his hands red. It should have looked ominous, but his cuffs were white, and the light dyed them as pink as his ridiculous strawberry-roan horse.

"There will be no helpful magic tonight," said Crevan.

She gazed at the pink cuffs and said nothing.

"By rights, I should accuse you of cheating," said Crevan. "Those were *your* tasks, not some bearish familiar's."

Rhea lifted her eyes. "You never said I had to do the tasks alone. And if we're speaking of cheating, the orchard path didn't vanish on its own."

He gave a short little laugh. Rhea suspected it was covering up anger. *No, I'm not mad. I thought it was funny. Didn't you hear me laughing? What makes you think you could make me angry?*

She abandoned any thought of asking what he planned to take from her. It would give him too much power over her to know that she wondered. She clasped her hands behind her back so that he would not see how she twisted her fingers together.

Crevan picked up a card from the book stand. It was folded into thirds and sealed with wax. "Tonight, you will go to the old well. When you get there, unseal this note and follow the orders. This one time, you must return *after* sunrise."

Rhea felt a flicker of relief that there was not a time limit, and immediately hated herself for it.

Do I really think he would make it easier? And even if he did, why should I be grateful that he's made the rules of his stupid little game easier on me?

"How many times are we going to do this?" she asked, digging her nails into her palm.

He raised an eyebrow and smiled.

And now he's happy again. Lovely.

"What if I told you this was the last task?" he asked.

She met his eyes squarely. "I don't know. Are you going to tell me that?"

His laugh this time was all amusement.

He likes to be challenged, thought Rhea, *but only when it's obvious that it's futile. He finds defiance funny, as long as you're still playing his game.*

It occurred to her that knowing this might be useful, if all went ill and she wound up married to him and trapped in this vast house with his growing collection of wives.

That was so grim a thought that she missed his next words. Then he held out the envelope to her, and she concentrated enough to take it.

"Don't open it until you reach the well," he said. "Or you will fail at once."

She nodded and left without asking permission.

Chapter Twenty-One

"The old well?" said Maria. "It's not far at all. Not like the graveyard. Go to the end of the orchard, where the two apple trees have grown together."

Rhea nodded and touched the note in her pocket. It felt vaguely oily. She took her hand away.

"Perhaps it'll be an easy one," she said.

Maria looked at her.

"I know," Rhea said, bowing her head, and slipped out of the kitchen.

She looked in vain for the hedgehog. It did not come out to greet her, and after lingering by the lamb's ears for a few moments, she continued on.

Perhaps it will find me. For all I know, it'll ride in at the last moment on dragonback and save me from whatever idiocy Crevan has planned for me.

It was a short walk. Compared with her two previous tasks, it seemed to take no time at all. She stepped off the path and picked her way through the grass, where the fallen apples were rotting quietly under the leaves.

She came abreast of the two apple trees that were wrapped around each other like lovers, and there was the well.

It was a short stone well with a metal crossbeam. There was no bucket or handle, and ferns grew in the gaps in the stone.

Sylvie was sitting on the edge of the well, which yawned black and cold behind her.

Rhea felt her stomach turn over with sudden dread.

The blind woman turned her head when Rhea approached and said, "Ingeth? Is that you?"

"No," said Rhea, "it's me."

"Oh," said Sylvie. "Good. Ingeth led me out here, but I'm afraid I didn't bring my stick. I'm not so good out of doors without it." She gave a small wisp of a laugh.

Rhea suddenly felt that she had not nearly needled Ingeth enough earlier.

Sylvie smiled in her direction. The wind tugged at a frayed end of the cloth around her eyes.

"I'll take you back in," said Rhea. "Just a moment . . ."

She dipped her hand into her pocket and unfolded the note. There was the faintest hint of a spark as she broke the wax seal. The silver ring burned on her finger.

There were two words written on it.

Kill her.

Rhea looked at them for a moment. She read them five or six times, but they did not change, and in truth, she hadn't expected them to.

Then she laughed, one short, painful laugh, and felt the knot in her stomach unclench.

Rhea had expected, when she finally failed a task, to be consumed with dread, to fall down weeping, to faint or scream or shriek like a child. Instead, what she felt was the first cousin to relief.

She had failed. It was over now. Whatever terrible thing was going to happen was out of her hands now, and she could stop playing Crevan's ridiculous game and focus on doing something useful, like running away or killing him or helping Maria and Sylvie.

She crumpled the note up and tossed it into the black mouth of the well. Her heart felt strangely light as she watched it disappear.

Perhaps I could simply walk up and stab him in the face. I wonder if anyone's tried that?

A little breeze sighed through the ruined orchard. Rhea could see Sylvie shiver.

She pulled off her cloak and tucked it around the blind woman's shoulders. "Come on," she said. "Let's get you home."

The return journey took longer. Sylvie tucked her arm through Rhea's, and they walked arm in arm through the grass. Rhea stumbled more often than Sylvie. "I'm sorry," she said when a ruined apple turned underfoot. "I don't know who's leading who."

Sylvie smiled. "It's all right," she said. "I wouldn't know which way to go without you."

They reached the path. Rhea glanced down toward the clearing where the golem wife hung beside the pool. *Whatever happens, I must figure out some way to free her as well.*

The going was easier now, but Rhea did not walk any faster than she needed to. The moon was just barely over the trees, and they were stepping into their own shadows, though Sylvie could not see it.

"I was beautiful once," said Sylvie quietly.

Rhea glanced at her.

"I'm not boasting," said Sylvie. "I was beautiful. I came from a land . . . oh, a long way away, I think. Everyone here is very dark, but we were all very pale. Lord Crevan came there and courted me. It was a long time ago."

"It's all right," said Rhea, because Sylvie's face was anguished. *Does she remember that other people can see her expressions?*

Sylvie shook her head. "It wasn't strange," she said. "That he made an offer, I mean. In my country, we aren't . . . we aren't nobles and peasants in the same way. Maria says it's different here, but in my country, lords marry beautiful women all the time. I don't want you to think badly of my parents."

"I don't," said Rhea, who hadn't thought of them at all.

"Good. They meant well." She sighed. "They didn't think it was odd . . ."

"Mine did," said Rhea, stepping on her shadow's heels. "Lords don't marry peasants here. They knew it was strange, but they couldn't do anything about it. You can't stop a lord doing what he wants. If you try . . . well . . . bad things happen."

Sylvie nodded.

The edge of the gardens came into view, and Rhea quickened her pace a little. "We're almost there."

Sylvie leaned her head against Rhea's shoulder and said, very quietly, "Be careful. Maria's afraid, but she's also excited. I can hear it in her voice. She thinks something's going to happen." Doubt crept into her voice. "She's not wicked, no matter what people say about witches. But she can be ruthless if she has to be. I love her, but it's true."

Rhea let out her breath in a long sigh. *She seems less befuddled out here . . . or perhaps if you live in a house where you are powerless, it is safer to seem harmless and befuddled. And she's not saying anything I haven't already considered.*

"Thank you," said Rhea.

Sylvie straightened. The moonlight made silver glitter of her hair.

"You're still beautiful," said Rhea, not quite sure whether she was telling a kind lie or not.

Sylvie smiled and shook her head. "Thank you," she said. "It shouldn't matter anymore. But it still does."

* * *

Maria took one look at them as they came through the door and drew in her breath as if she'd been struck a blow.

Her eyes sought Rhea's. Rhea shook her head slightly, settling Sylvie into a chair. *Not now.*

Maria nodded.

"Ingeth took me outside. Rhea walked me back," said Sylvie, sounding pleased and somewhat childlike again.

Rhea glanced down at her, her suspicions confirmed.

She may not be the smartest woman, but she's smart enough to play dumb. I don't think it's completely an act—I'm pretty sure she's not entirely all there—but she's also not doing anything that might make herself look like a threat. Hmm.

It was interesting. Rhea could admire it, in the abstract. From battling swans, she had learned to fight back or to run away. It had not previously occurred to her to dress up like a rock or a tree or some other part of the landscape so the swan would swim past her.

Bit late to start that with Crevan . . . besides, it hasn't worked out too well for Sylvie. He was willing to let her die to see if I'd pass his test.

Maria fussed over Sylvie, getting her another cup of tea. Rhea turned toward the door.

"Tea?" asked Maria.

Rhea shook her head. "I have to talk to Himself."

Now, before I lose my courage. Now, while I still feel a little bit invincible.

She was almost to the doorway when the house started rocking and the floor began falling away.

Rhea clung to the doorframe, glanced over her shoulder, and said, "I guess it's midnight."

She had a better view of the process this time. The sight of the baseboards descending directly into the bedrock was still profoundly absurd.

More unsettling, the tiles that stayed in place appeared to be hanging in empty air. There was nothing underneath them. The end table with the flower arrangement on it hung suspended over the abyss.

"How does that *work*, anyway?" asked Rhea.

Maria came up behind her. "It has to do with the way the manor house touches many places at many times. That's how the roads got so muddled. The clock wife, when she's angry, pulls the house to a place and time where there's nothing underneath it."

Rhea turned her head to stare at Maria. "She can *do* that?"

Maria shrugged. "More or less. There's a technical explanation, but it would mostly be of interest to witches and sorcerers. And possibly clock makers."

"Is she trapped in there? Like the golem wife?"

The cook watched the tiles fly up out of the pit, like white stone birds. Her voice was low and rapid. "The inside of the clock is different. He has no power there, so he stays out of it. When she shakes the house, his power is weak for a little while. I must ask, if the chance comes, would you be willing . . ."

She broke off. Rhea turned and saw the last tiles fitting themselves into place.

That's interesting. If I can catch her when the floor falls again, maybe she can answer some of my questions.

Rhea stifled a snort. The entire process lasted such a short time. *Well. One question, then. I wonder what I should ask?*

How do I kill Crevan?

No, don't be ridiculous. If she knew how to kill him, she'd have done it herself already. I doubt she'd even think twice about it.

At this point, I wouldn't, either . . .

She tested the first step with her toes, then the second. The tiles did not move.

"It's not me you want . . . ," she whispered, glancing across the room at the clock.

The minute hand shuddered past midnight. Rhea took a deep breath and strode out across the seemingly solid floor.

She found Crevan's study easily enough. The path had embedded itself in her mind, which was a good thing, because Ingeth was nowhere to be found.

After she left Sylvie out in the orchard like that, I hope she never shows up again . . .

She did not knock.

Crevan was sitting behind the desk with candles burning around him. He was wearing white again. He looked clean and elegant, and Rhea was reminded once more of the swan from the millrace.

Very noble, very beautiful, and vicious down to the bone.

Crevan looked up as she entered, and for one moment, naked surprise flickered across his face.

"It's not sunrise," he said blankly.

Rhea stared at him.

He thought I was going to sit out there until sunrise? Why would anyone do that?

And then, a second, teasing little thought said, *He didn't know I was on my way to his study. Is his magic not working? Perhaps because the clock wife shook the house just now? Or maybe he isn't all-seeing after all . . .*

As she watched, the urbane mask slipped down over Crevan's face, smoothing the lines. "Miss Rhea. You're back sooner than I expected."

"I've failed your test," said Rhea shortly. "Now what?"

Crevan shook his head, smiling. It seemed to Rhea that the smile was just a trifle forced, but perhaps it was the light. "Have you? Such a shame."

"That I'm not a killer? Not really." Rhea folded her arms.

"Aren't you?" asked Crevan. His smile broadened. "Surely, you must have thought about it for a moment. The way out of all your difficulties . . ."

Oh, Lady of Stones. He really thought I was going to sit there until sunrise, wondering if I should shove her into the well. He thought this was some kind of terrible mental torture.

"My mother raised me not to push other people down wells," said Rhea. "It's surprisingly easy, if you don't get into the habit of it. What happens now?"

He rose from behind the desk, laughing. "Goodness, Miss Rhea. Perhaps contemplating murder agrees with you. We shall be wed, of course. That was always the price of failure."

"When?" said Rhea, determined not to rise to the bait and waste this strange, heady courage that had her in its grip.

"At once," said Crevan. "I shall arrange the priest. The viscount will attend, as he has so kindly given me permission to wed one of his tenants."

Rhea would never have admitted it, but she felt a brief spasm of hope. Not that the viscount would take the side of a miller's daughter, never that, but viscounts could not be produced out of thin air.

He'll have to arrange for his friend to show up. I should get at least a week—perhaps even a month. That's a long time. I can get away . . .

"And your dear parents, of course," Crevan added smoothly. "They shall certainly wish to see their daughter again. And I will be most delighted to see *them* again."

His eyes held hers as he spoke, and his smile did not flicker once.

Hope withered and died.

"Was that a threat?" she demanded, knowing full well that it was.

Crevan grinned down at her. "I misjudged you," he said, "when I said that you weren't clever. You still aren't, but I believe that perhaps you could learn."

He turned away from her, toward his desk, and for lack of other options, Rhea took out the kitchen knife and stabbed him in the back.

It was easier than stabbing the dog monster, she'd give it that. And the knife actually went in a little way, which was very gratifying, right up until the point where it hit something hard and stopped going in, and she tried to yank on it, and his shirt got bunched up around it, and the knife came out, and Crevan shrieked and whipped around and threw her into the wall.

The back of her head struck first, so all she saw were dazzling white flashes, and the room suddenly went very dark. Then it occurred to her that she couldn't breathe, and she thought, *Oh, I've hit a wall, how interesting.*

Crevan pawed at his back, cursing. He looked like a man trying to scratch an itchy spot between his shoulders. Rhea found this distantly amusing, except for the bit where she couldn't get any air in her lungs and the room still seemed strangely dark and fuzzy around the edges.

"Ingeth!" bellowed Crevan. *"Ingeth!"*

Ingeth darted into the room. She looked from Crevan to Rhea and started toward Rhea.

"Not her," growled Crevan. "The little bitch stabbed me!"

Ingeth's eyes went big and round, and Rhea laughed, which was a bad idea because she couldn't even breathe. She made a hoarse hacking sound instead.

Things went a bit gray for a moment.

Her surroundings came into focus once more when the world moved around her. Crevan had picked her up by the front of her blouse, pulling the collar tight around her throat.

"You have to be of reasonably sound mind in order to say the words," he told her. "After that, if you're a drooling simpleton, it won't matter in the least. I suggest you think about *that.*"

Rhea croaked something. She would have liked it to be defiant, but it was actually "Can't . . . breathe . . ."

The world lurched again. He carried her for the five steps to the corridor and then dropped her, hard.

The world went thud, and then it went away entirely.

Chapter Twenty-Two

"Well," said Maria. "Well, well. That wasn't smart, as much as I appreciate the sentiment. How's your head?"

"It hurts," said Rhea, tentatively feeling the back of her skull.

"Of course it hurts. You keep poking it." Maria handed her a mug of tea. "How's your vision? Seeing double? Bright shine around the edges of things? Ghosts of birds?"

"No, not anymore. I'm—ghosts of birds?"

"Well, you never know your luck." Maria took a slurp of tea. "Let me know if any show up. It's not likely you're the Kingfisher Saint, but things happen."

"W-what?"

"Never you mind. And what were you thinking, stabbing him like that?"

"I was hoping I'd kill him," said Rhea. Her lungs felt raw. The tea helped her throat, though, and perhaps there wasn't much to be done about her lungs.

After she had fainted—or whatever it was—Ingeth had either gone to fetch Maria or Maria had come on her own. Rhea had roused as she was being steered down the stairs by Maria, and she'd allowed herself to be helped groggily into a kitchen chair.

"That's not the way to kill him," said Maria. "You'll need the clock wife's help."

Rhea looked up, startled. Her head rang with the motion, and she held her head in her hands, elbows propped on the kitchen table.

"Don't worry," said Maria. "Himself is gone, off to the city to fetch the priest and some of his high-and-mighty friends. We can speak freely, at least for a little while, and you're not going to sleep until I'm sure that crack on the head hasn't addled your wits."

Rhea exhaled. She had so many questions, and suddenly only one seemed important.

"When will he be back?"

"End of the week, he said—and with orders to see that all is ready by then, if you please. Although how he expects me to pull a wedding feast together by myself, I surely do not know." She glared into her mug.

After a moment, she added, "He left you a note."

Rhea put her forehead down on the table and let out a single dry sob, almost a laugh. "Of course he did. He's very fond of notes."

"Perhaps he's afraid you'll stab him again," said Maria.

Rhea looked up, startled, and caught a wicked gleam in the cook's eye.

It wrung a laugh out of her, not much different than the sob. "Where's the note?"

Maria slid it over.

It was very short, four lines only. Rhea dared to hope that he had written it in haste.

> *It will do no good to lie and say that I am not disappointed by your behavior, Miss Rhea. Still, I have chosen to attribute your actions to an overabundance of nerves. I shall return for our wedding in one week.*

I suggest that you use the time to reflect on the behavior proper to a girl of your station.

Crevan

Rhea thought about getting angry. She actually thought about it, about letting the words sink in and dwelling on how wrong they were. She could taste the hot wash of fury that would rush through her as she read over those terrible words again and again, and there was no denying that it would feel good to be so angry.

Reluctantly, she pushed the anger away.

It would not help. He was not here. And she had to put the time she had to the best possible use.

"Maria," said Rhea, gathering her thoughts, "you have to tell me everything."

"Ask," said Maria. "What answers I have, I'll give."

Rhea nodded. "He, he takes something from each wife, doesn't he? He took your magic and Sylvie's sight—"

Maria nodded. "Aye, indeed. Something from each. He's a sorcerer, you understand, and he works by contracts. Most of his kind make contracts with demons, but Himself eventually figured out that a marriage contract works as well. He just had to find women who have things he wants. Sign the paper that says you're wed, and you're in his power—though he's careful with how he uses it."

"*How* does it work?"

Maria shook her head. "I am—I was—a witch, child, not a sorcerer. I imagine they do it the way I did witching, which is to say that it can be easily practiced but not easily learned."

"But people have been marrying magical folk for years—centuries—and I've never heard of anything like *this*."

Maria sighed. "It's a perversion of the contract, child. My first husband was a sweet man, and when he signed his *X* next to mine on the page, he would never have dreamed of doing such a thing, even if he had the power."

Rhea turned the silver ring on her finger grimly.

Maria held out her hand. An identical ring gleamed in the lamplight.

"As near as I can tell," she said, "he gives you his name—whether you want it or not—and in return he can take something from you. One thing. He only ever takes one. It may be that if he took more, he'd have to give more."

Rhea considered this. "Could we use that somehow?"

Maria shook her head. "If you're looking for a way to break the contract, I don't know one. You'd need a demon or a barrister to answer that."

Rhea took a deep breath. "What does he want from *me*?"

The other woman grew very interested in her tea.

"Maria!"

"I don't know," she admitted. "I thought perhaps, you being so young, it was your youth he wanted, but I don't *know*."

Rhea took a deep breath. It seemed to get caught up somewhere inside her chest.

"He can do that?" she asked.

Maria shrugged. "Maybe. If he can take one wife's death or another wife's will, what can't he do?"

Rhea put her face in hands. She did not feel young. She felt about a thousand years old, and Maria, who was easily three or four times her age, did not seem to have any answers for her.

"He doesn't usually *keep* the gifts, you understand," said Maria. "He kept mine, though." There was a perverse pride in her voice as she said it. "Without mine, he'd not have half the power to keep the house bent to his will. And all those golems—he makes them with my magic. I could do it, too, but I was a defter hand with the needle, and I would never have done it to a *living* thing."

She shook herself. "He gave the rest away—or traded them anyway. A lot of fingers in a lot of pies."

"Gave them away?" asked Rhea, even more confused. "How do you give away somebody's *sight*?"

"Magic," said Maria. "I know that one, for she came in here in a hood and jesses. He gave Sylvie's sight to the Eagle King's daughter, hatched blind from the egg."

Rhea blinked a few times.

I'm hearing things. I was hit harder than I thought. I'll be seeing those ghosts of birds before I know it.

"Eagle King," she said.

"From the farthest west. Turns out Eagles won't let you inherit if you're blind. Himself offered to fix her up, so he married Sylvie and traded her sight away a few months later."

Rhea fisted her hands in her hair.

If hedgehogs can summon slugs to save me and bears can be familiars and Crevan can exist at all, I suppose there can be Eagle Kings.

"And Ingeth's voice?" she asked dully.

"I don't know what became of it." Maria shook her head. "Nor do I know which poor soul was dealt the clock wife's death. I imagine he killed a rival of his, or someone powerful." She paused, tapping a finger against her lips. "As far as Lady Elegans goes . . . well, there was a great lord in the city whose daughter was deathly ill at about the time the lady died. Even the boy who delivers the food was full of the news. She made an amazing recovery, they said, almost magic, and the lady died without a mark on her. But I've got no proof. People die and don't die all the time. Might be coincidence. Still, there's enough witch blood left in me to get the wind up."

"What about the golem wife?"

Maria poured more tea. "Was a young man here, a few years back. Nice young fellow, but no spine at all. Not even enough to question why a sorcerer would live alone with a handful of women." She gazed at Rhea over the rim of her cup. "Set upon by his relations, he was, and him a prince of some far-off land. Himself married poor Hester a fortnight later and took her will within the week. And the prince went back to his own country with his jaw square and a flame in his heart. He didn't get that courage out of a bottle."

Rhea pushed her tea away. "So maybe he'll give away whatever he takes from me," she said. She didn't know why that would make her feel worse, but somehow it did. It was one thing for someone to covet something you had and steal it, but for that person to hold it so cheaply that they would give it away . . . "He just, just figures someone else should have it."

"Oh, aye," said Maria. "Considers himself a great humanitarian. He's helping the goodly and the great, and what are we after all?" She chuckled humorlessly. "Doesn't hurt that the great owe him favors afterward, either."

"And the clock wife—"

"Hello, Ingeth," said Maria, too loudly. "I see you skulking by the door. Come in if you want something to drink."

Ingeth came in. She had her wrists drawn up against her chest and would not look at Rhea.

"Himself's gone," said Maria. "You know it better than I do. You can come sit in here if you want, instead of dancing attendance."

Ingeth took a few steps forward as Maria filled a mug for her. She looked like some strange praying mantis, not like a person at all.

Pity and rage warred on Rhea's tongue, and when she finally spoke, she still wasn't sure which had won. "You brought Sylvie out to the well. Why would you *do* that?"

She expected a glower, but instead, the other woman snatched up the mug of tea and hurried out the door.

"Easy now," said Maria. "I make no excuses for Ingeth, but don't lose sight of the real enemy."

"The task was to kill Sylvie," said Rhea. "Ingeth brought her out there. I was supposed to kill her." The world seemed to spin as she said it. Perhaps it was only her bruised skull.

The cook's breath hissed in between her teeth. "I might have known," she said. "Bitch. Not you. Ingeth. How dare she? Taking Sylvie out in the middle of the night!"

It seemed to Rhea that Maria was angry about the wrong thing. "But, Maria, I was supposed to *kill* her!"

Maria rolled her eyes and poured herself more tea. "Which you had no chance of doing. Even Himself knew that, and he doesn't know half as much about human hearts as he thinks he does."

Rhea took a long slug of tea, not sure if she should be angry or not. Fortunately Maria was angry enough for both of them.

"Sylvie could have caught her death out there. She's not well. She was never strong, but he shattered her health when he took her eyes. She's not even thirty, you know."

Rhea hadn't known. Sylvie's fragility made her seem very old. Perhaps it was the paleness of her hair. Only the very old had hair that color, in Rhea's experience.

"I do my best to take care of her, but there's only so much to be done. It's hard when he takes things."

"How bad is it?" Rhea asked.

Maria exhaled. "Bad enough," she admitted. "I nearly died. A witch's magic is like a witch's skin. Ripping it all off at once would kill most people. Sylvie's health broke. You've seen Hester—the golem wife." She turned her mug in her hands, worrying at a chip on the handle with her thumb. "I will say that he's gotten better at it. Ingeth was . . . pretty horrible, with her throat laid open like that, but she healed up fast."

Rhea had been thinking of the marriage to Crevan as something horrible and possibly fatal. It had not occurred to her that it would also be excruciating. She bent her neck and set her forehead against the scarred wood of the table.

"I can't run," she said miserably. "I tried. The white road is full of monsters. Devils. I don't know what."

Maria nodded. "Most sorcerers have them," she said. "Things they called up when they were young and foolish, then couldn't send back to wherever they came from. They have to put them somewhere, but the beasts are always hungry, and they'll kill the sorcerer if they can." She pursed her lips. "Himself is cleverer than most," she admitted. "You can get to this manor any number of ways, but all the roads *out* of here lead to the white road, unless he sets it different. He took his failures and made them into his prison guards. There's no running for us. But you already knew that."

Rhea nodded. "If it was just my life on the line, I'd ruin the wedding. Yell *no!* when the priest asks if I'll marry this man. But he's threatening my parents. He'll kill them, take the mill, turn them out—oh, Maria, I can't!"

She began to cry, wretchedly, feeling as helpless as Sylvie.

Maria put a hand on her shoulder. After a few minutes, Rhea stopped.

If I have learned anything at all over this last week, it's that crying doesn't seem to help at all.

"Better?" asked Maria conversationally.

"A little."

"You're willing to kill him?" Her tone didn't change, still light, two women discussing nothing in particular.

"In a heartbeat," Rhea said and laughed painfully. "For all the good it will do me. I couldn't even stab him properly."

"I wasn't sure," said Maria quietly. "There's them as wouldn't, not even to save their own lives. And I didn't dare ask while he was here, unless the floor was falling." She took a deep breath. "We'll only get one chance, I expect."

Rhea looked up. The *we* warmed her a little. At least she wasn't in this alone. "One chance?"

"Like I said, the clock wife's no friend of his," said Maria. "She was never quite human, as near as I can tell, and it took most of the magic he stole from me to bind her into the clock." She snorted. "He was hoping to pull her power from her as well, I expect, but she was too much for him. In the end, her death was the only thing he could wrestle away from her."

A tile rattled in the next room, as if in acknowledgment.

"Into the clock you'll go, then," said Maria, nodding.

"Now?" asked Rhea. Her head was aching, but she forced herself to stand. "All right."

Maria pushed her back down. "No, not now, child. We'll wait until he returns. It will do us no good to release her *now*. We'll have her mad and rampaging and bringing the whole house down on us, and for what? He'll still be out there, and your parents may not fare too well when he finds out what happened. Nor Sylvie's for that matter—oh, yes, he's got that hold over her as well."

Rhea paused. "Mad and rampaging" did not sound promising. "Is she going to be very angry?"

"She's been trapped inside a clock, on the far side of time, where instants drag on for eternities, and she cannot even die because her own *death* was stolen from her. At a guess, she's pretty pissed, aye."

Rhea swallowed. "Is she going to listen to me?"

Maria swirled her tea and gazed at the ceiling—not as she did when Crevan was in his study, but in a way that said she was avoiding Rhea's eyes.

"Maria . . ."

The former witch sighed. "There's a good chance she'll kill you. I don't know how much awareness she has of what's going on out here. You may have to convince her you're no friend of Himself. Or she may know exactly who you are and what you're about, and you'll just have to give her the opening. Even I don't know what goes on inside that clock."

"Why me?" asked Rhea.

Thinking, *Why haven't you gone in yourself? Why haven't you sent Sylvie? Or the golem wife, who you said was so strong willed?*

Was Maria risking Rhea's life for something that she didn't dare do herself?

"She can be ruthless if she has to be," Sylvie had said.

Maria smiled faintly. "Because you might stand a chance. Things keep coming to your aid. And I can't go myself, because someone has to stand out here and hold the way."

Chapter Twenty-Three

The week dragged on, and yet it was over all too quickly. Each hour seemed to last for a thousand years, but then Rhea would find herself at the end of the day, unable to remember anything but flashes. *I did laundry, I weeded the flower bed, yes, the hedgehog came out of the garden and sat with me while I did it, but what else did I do, and how is a whole day gone?*

And another day would be over, and her wedding would move a little bit closer. And if Maria was correct, the end of her youth moved closer as well.

And here I was afraid he wanted a child . . . instead he's just going to suck the youth out of me.

I wonder if I'll die.

Would she suddenly find herself ninety years old? Or merely the same age as Crevan was now? Would Crevan keep her gift for himself, as he had kept Maria's?

That can't be right. All his noble friends would notice if he became that much younger.

She could not stop picturing herself as an old woman, hair whiter than Sylvie's, stooped over a cane. No matter how hard she tried to bury it, the image kept creeping back into her mind.

It did not help that she had little to do but think. She spent hours sitting with her back to the clock. Maria had suggested it. If the floor had not continued to fall each day at midnight, she would likely have slept there as well.

"Cuddle up to it," said Maria. "Give her a chance to notice you."

"It's a clock, not a kitten," said Rhea. "It's hard to cuddle with a clock."

"She was a bit catlike," said Maria thoughtfully, stirring the sauce for the evening's meal. "Mostly around the eyes. Not like a house cat, though. Or it may have been lizardlike, now that I think of it . . ."

Rhea stared at her.

"Don't give me that look, child. I told you she wasn't human."

"What was she?" asked Rhea faintly, wondering why she was even bothering to be surprised.

"Hell if I know. Something old. Something that liked flattery." She tasted the sauce and frowned. "Needs more salt."

"Where did she come from?"

"Up Sylvie's way, I think," said Maria, drying her hands on her apron. "Their lands aren't as settled as ours, and things come up from under the ice sometimes."

Sylvie, who was sitting at the table across from Rhea, nodded. She was rubbing beans between her fingers, separating out the small ones and the occasional pebbles. "There was a glacier not far from my town," she said. "Sometimes when the ice retreated in summer, things would melt out. You had to block the doors at night. They were always hungry."

Rhea blinked. "That sounds . . . unpleasant?"

Maria laughed, but Sylvie's expression turned thoughtful as she slid beans across the table. "Not really. You get used to things. It was just something you did in the summer—barring the doors and putting wunderclutter on them to confuse anything that might come by."

Ingeth stood in the doorway. It seemed to Rhea that the voiceless woman was often lurking around the edges these days, just within earshot.

In her more charitable moments, she wondered if Ingeth was attracted to their laughter. The rest of the time, she just figured the other woman was spying.

And why are we laughing and chatting anyway? We're like rats trapped in a hole, telling stories until the cat gets home again.

She knew the answer to that one, at least. *What other choice do we have? It will not get any less horrible if we spend all our time weeping . . .*

After Ingeth claimed a cup of tea and went away again, Rhea decided to ask Maria about it outright. "Why is Ingeth always lurking around?"

"She lives here," said Maria mildly. "I don't pretend to like her, but she doesn't have anywhere else to lurk."

Rhea sighed and rubbed her forehead.

Maria tasted the sauce again. "As for why she's lurking around us . . . Well, she was always one for finding fault, although she doesn't point it out as much these days."

"I hate her," said Rhea angrily. "I hate Crevan, but she's helping him, and that's almost worse."

Sylvie made a small, agitated noise. "Don't say hate," she begged. "Hate's a sin. We're only allowed to hate evil things."

"If Crevan's not evil, then what is?"

Sylvie fell silent.

Maria moved the pot off the stove. "She helps him because she believes she is being punished," she said. "It is all she has left."

Rhea frowned. "I don't understand."

Maria sighed. "It is sometimes easier to be punished for something than it is to be a victim of random cruelty. As long as Ingeth can tell herself that her voice was taken from her because she committed some sin, then she has some control of it, you understand? Otherwise it was simply a terrible thing that happened. And if terrible things are allowed to happen to people that don't deserve them, then the world is terrible and random and cruel. Which it is," she added, pointing the spoon in Rhea's direction, "but there's not much comfort in *that*."

There was silence for a moment, except for the tapping of Sylvie sorting the beans.

Rhea rubbed her forehead. It seemed terribly pointless . . . and yet, hadn't she done something akin to that herself? Playing Crevan's game as if there were rules and a point to it all, instead of acknowledging that Crevan was simply a madman and there was no way to win against him.

"But why would she *help* him?" she asked. That was the part that made no sense at all.

"Because he is the tool of her punishment. And if there is no point to it all, then she has been helping a monster for years. So she keeps doing what she started, digging herself in deeper, hoping that she is helping an instrument of divine judgment and fearing that she isn't."

Rhea propped her chin in her hand and said, "That's completely mad."

Maria gave a vast shrug. "People are sometimes." She swept the beans off the table and into another pot. "Thank you, Sylvie."

Sylvie nodded. Rhea could tell that the conversation had distressed her. Perhaps Ingeth wasn't the only person hoping that there was some point to it all.

"Tell me about the glaciers," she said, turning toward Sylvie. "I've never seen one."

Sylvie smiled, and for a moment, it was easy to see how she had been considered beautiful. "Oh, they're marvelous! Great white sheets from far away, and then you get closer—carefully, because they make you fall down sometimes—and there are colors inside. Twisting blues and grays and greens and every possible shade of white. Sometimes they look like glass." She laughed a little. "Sometimes they're a churned-up mess of rocks and trees, of course . . ."

"And sometimes monsters come out?"

"Well, yes. Sometimes there are monsters." Sylvie leaned forward. "Don't they have monsters where you live?"

"Let me tell you about swans . . . ," said Rhea, and the conversation turned to other things.

A few minutes later, as Sylvie was explaining ice fishing, Rhea leaned back in her chair. Out of the corner of her eye, she saw Ingeth in the shadow of the doorway, but when she turned her head, the silent woman hurried away.

When Rhea could not sit still for a moment longer, she walked. She went from one side of the manor house to the other, opening doors and closing them again.

The door to Crevan's study was locked. Rhea considered getting a chair and trying to beat it down, but she thought it was just possible that he would sense it if someone had broken into the study and come back early. That might mean her wedding would be early, and that was exactly the sort of thing that she was trying to avoid.

She found Sylvie's room, in a set of suites identical to the one where her room was located. The furniture was mismatched and shabby, but comfortable.

She never found Maria's.

There was a portrait gallery near the top of the house. It had long rows of windows, and Rhea thought they might be some of the ones she had seen from outside.

The oldest portraits were vanishing in a haze of dark varnish, but the nameplates said "Elegans."

"Did he marry Lady Elegans to get her house?" Rhea asked Maria, when she returned at last to the kitchens.

"Well . . . in a manner of speaking," said Maria, rubbing her chin. "He had the house already, you understand. The Eleganses built this place, near as I can tell, but the Crevans got it away from them years ago. I don't know what happened to the Eleganses. The lady didn't have more'n a drop of witch blood in her, but somebody way back when had to have built the house." She shrugged. "Anyhow, he came along asking to marry me—and more the fool I for believing him, but he was a flatterer and said how he wanted to learn from me." She snorted. "Well, he learned a lot, I'll give him that. How to wring the magic out of a witch, for one thing."

She slapped a ball of dough down and began kneading it fiercely. "He tried a fair number of things with my magic," she said over her shoulder. "He set up the white road with it, for one thing. But the house didn't work as well for him, and there weren't so many ways in and out. I think—and this is only a guess, you understand—he married the lady to try and buy his way into the house's good graces and convince it he was an Elegans."

"Did it work?" asked Rhea.

"More or less. He got a lot better with the roads after he married her anyhow." The former witch shrugged. "A house this old isn't alive like you or me, but it's not quite dead, either. I daresay it could decide to help him if it thought it should."

"Do you think there's a way out?" asked Rhea. "On the roads?"

Maria shook her head. "Not that I've found," she said. "And I tried a few times, once I could stand up again, after my magic was taken. You wouldn't think I could fit through a window, would you?"

Rhea paused, torn between honesty and tact.

Maria laughed. "I can if I have to," she said. "For all the good it did me. Never got more than a quarter mile before I hit the white road again. I could have stayed in the house and saved myself the trouble."

* * *

There were four days left.

There were three days left.

There were two days left.

And then it was the last day, and Rhea spent it with her back pressed against the clock, drinking unending cups of tea. She could not eat.

"Starving yourself won't help," said Maria.

"I'm not starving myself," said Rhea. "I'm sorry, Maria. I'm trying, I just can't." When she took a bite, the food felt like thick glue in her mouth. Chewing took effort, and her stomach was clenched like a fist.

"All right," said Maria, searching her face. She took the plate away. "I'll make you some soup. It'll go down a bit easier anyway."

The soup helped.

Why am I eating soup? This is insane. I'm marrying a monster tomorrow—probably. He didn't give a time. Maybe I've got another day, maybe even two . . .

She turned her head, so that her cheek lay against the wooden case, and breathed deeply.

Sometimes she dozed for a bit, leaning against the clock. She thought that she heard a tapping once or twice, like the tapping she had followed through the rooms days earlier. When she came a little more awake, she was not sure if she had dreamed it or not.

Maria, standing in the doorway, cleared her throat and said, "The dress has come."

Rhea pressed her forehead to her knees and gave a single sob of laughter. *A dress! Oh, Lady of Stones!*

"I know," said Maria.

"I'll cut it up. I'll throw *it* down the well. I'll let the hedgehog at it."

"And then you'll put him on his guard," said Maria, "and if all goes ill, you'll risk getting married in an old apron."

"I thought if all went ill, I'd be dead."

"That, too."

Rhea lifted her face. "You're actually suggesting I wear the dress?"

"I'm suggesting that if you're going to bring hell down upon someone's head, you might as well dress for the occasion. Come into the kitchen. It's the wrong size, I'm sure, but I've got my pins. We should be able to figure something out."

Leaving the clock was strangely difficult. She didn't know if sitting there was doing anything, but it felt more like *doing something* than anything else did. Even if all it was actually doing was etching a red welt in her skin where the hinge dug into her back.

She pulled herself up and headed into the kitchen.

The dress was laid out on the table in front of Sylvie, who sat running her hands over the soft fabric. "A wedding," she said, apparently without irony. "I love weddings."

Maria and Rhea exchanged meaningful glances over her head.

"They were so wonderful, back home," said Sylvie. "The bride would have flowers—you were only allowed to wear flowers, not jewelry. And we would have the ceremony, and then they'd jump over a broomstick—you had to do that, it was traditional. And everyone would cry." She sighed. "I miss them."

"One of these days," said Maria, "when things are—ah—different, I'll take you to another wedding."

Sylvie smiled. "I'd like that. It wouldn't matter if I couldn't see. It might be easier actually. Some of those grooms were not very handsome. You still had to say, 'Oh, what a lovely couple!' even if one of them had a nose like a squashed frog."

She reached out and patted Rhea's hand. "I know it's not like a real wedding for you," she said kindly. "I'm sorry."

"It's all right," said Rhea automatically, even though it wasn't.

"But at least you have a lovely dress. Everyone should have one."

Rhea looked glumly at the dress.

It was red, the color of weddings, a stronger shade than the red dress that Crevan had given her as an engagement gift, several weeks and several lifetimes ago. It was the color of scarlet roses. It hung in stiff folds that cascaded to the floor and looked to be several sizes too big.

Maria muttered to herself, sweeping up a handful of pins. "At least it's too large and not too small. Easier to take in than take out . . ."

Rhea found herself stripped down to her shift in the middle of the kitchen. She stared at the ceiling. The woodworms had been in the beams, leaving slender tracks along the surface of the wood. Maria moved around her, pinning and tucking and grumbling.

The hedgehog trundled in from the garden, took one look at the proceedings, gave an audible *chuff!* of disgust, and trundled out again.

"Slits," muttered Maria, taking up the scissors. "It's a crime to do this to good fabric, but you need to be able to walk. I've never understood why they make dresses like horse hobbles."

"Don't you?" asked Rhea. Her head felt light and very far away.

Maria's hands paused for a moment. "Sometimes people talk so they don't have to say anything," she said dryly. "It's not nice to call them out on it. Now lift your arms, child, and make sure you can move them."

Rhea fled back to the clock as soon as she could.

The wood under her back was warm. The glass was cold. She braced her feet on the floor and pushed herself against the clock case, half hoping to sink into the side. *Is that how it works? How am I going to go into the clock? I hope Maria knows, because even if we open the door, I'm going to walk in and get a face full of gears, and what good will that do? I suppose it's possible Crevan won't marry me if I'm all over blood and gear marks, but if I could rely on that, I'd just cut my face up and go home.*

It seemed to her that the clock was shifting a little bit, making a tiny hollow for her body. Perhaps it was her own flesh that was doing the shifting. Perhaps this was all a nightmare, and she would wake up, and it would still be seven days to the wedding.

I am no longer hoping to wake up back home. Now I would be glad for a little more time.

And night fell, and then there was no more time left.

* * *

Rhea sensed it the moment Crevan arrived. The house seemed to shift just a little. It was probably her imagination, but the air suddenly seemed hot and stale, and the walls seemed to press in against the room.

The clock shuddered behind her, and a tile on the far corner of the floor clattered into darkness.

Perhaps it wasn't her imagination after all.

Rhea got to her feet. There was no point in going back to her bedroom. The dress was in there. She had tried to sleep earlier, but her eyes had refused to stop staring at the back of the door, at the dress the color of roses.

It would be better if it were blood-colored. That way I could feel . . . I don't know, dangerous.

It is hard to feel dangerous in a dress the color of rose petals.

She had gone back to the clock and curled up in front of it, almost dozing, her forehead resting against her knees. It was not comfortable, and yet it helped her understand why Maria slept sitting at the kitchen table.

Now Crevan was in the house.

Well.

If he was in the house, she would not be.

Let him send Ingeth if he wants me so badly.

She got to her feet and patted the clock absently, as if it truly were a cat. They were in this together, all of them. Rhea, Maria, the clock wife. The golem wife and Sylvie. Perhaps even Ingeth, though it strained Rhea's compassion to include her.

She went through the door of the kitchen, and a moment later the floor fell behind her. And that was odd, she thought, because it was twenty minutes after midnight.

Was she waiting for me to leave before dropping the floor? Does she know that I'm there?

That was a good thing, or a bad thing, or perhaps simply a thing. She was beyond knowing.

Maria sat at the table, elbow propped on the edge. Rhea did not disturb her. She pushed the garden door open a crack and slipped through.

The air was cold and bracing enough to rouse her from her thoughts. She made her way to the wall and slid down it, no longer willing to sit without something at her back after all the time she'd spent with the clock.

The hedgehog found her a few moments later. It made a small noise and climbed into her lap.

"You should be eating slugs," Rhea whispered, stroking the little animal's quills.

It shrugged.

"Whatever . . . whatever happens tomorrow—" Rhea began, and her voice cracked, which she hadn't expected. She waited for a little bit, then tried again. "Whatever happens, be careful. This is a bad place. Maria will feed you, but you should try to get away."

The hedgehog gave her one of its annoyed looks.

"I never really understood why you came along at all," said Rhea. She tried to laugh, and it came out half a sob. "I'm just . . . glad you did."

It shook its head and slid off her lap. As it trundled away into the darkened garden, she felt tears slick her face.

It was easier to cry in front of the hedgehog than it was to cry in front of Maria. Still . . .

Sobbing in a dark garden all night won't get me anywhere.

She took a deep breath, felt it catch, held it anyway. Then another, then another.

The hedgehog tapped her knee.

She looked down.

It was holding a large, soft leaf.

"Lamb's ear, huh?" asked Rhea, taking the leaf. She wiped her face with it and tried to smile.

The hedgehog sighed. It curled up against her ankle, and together they waited out the long and final night.

Chapter Twenty-Four

She woke late in the morning. There was dew soaking her clothes, and her neck was stiff.

"Rhea?" asked a voice hesitantly.

Rhea looked up. There was a woman standing there, a woman who looked very familiar, someone she knew from somewhere—

Oh.

"Mother?" said Rhea.

Her mother went down to her knees, ignoring the fact that she was wearing her very finest clothes. "Rhea . . . ? Why are you sleeping out here?"

Rhea could not think of an answer. The moment drew out too long, and her mother's face shifted, the tiny muscles around her mouth going slack and old. Her skin, normally so dark, had gray undertones of worry.

"It's gone wrong, hasn't it, honey?" her mother whispered. "It's not good, is it?"

Rhea shook her head mutely.

Her mother held out her arms, and Rhea tumbled into them.

It was not a comforting hug, but one of fear and resolve. "I told your father," her mother whispered. "I told him you were gone too long, that something had gone bad, but he said we had no choice."

"You didn't," said Rhea, finding her voice. "You didn't. You couldn't have known."

"I knew," said her mother.

"You would have lost the mill."

"To hell with the mill," growled her mother—her sweet, beloved mother, who scolded for any curses stronger than *darn*.

Rhea laughed jerkily, feeling her chest unknot a little.

"We'll get you out of here," her mother said. "We'll go now. If we must, we'll move."

Rhea shook her head, pushing away. The reality of the situation was still there, looming huge and grim before her, and her mother was no match for Crevan. "No," she said. "No, we can't. No—I mean *really*. He's a sorcerer, Mother, a bad one. You can't get out of this place unless he lets you."

Her mother absorbed this in silence.

"I . . . I can't tell you much more," said Rhea. "He might be listening. He can—it's a thing he can do, listening. I'm sorry." The expression on her mother's face made her heart ache again. "I have to do this."

Her mother reached out and caught her upper arms, her face fierce. "If you're doing this to protect the mill—"

"And you," said Rhea miserably. "And all of us. It's not just me. We can't get away. There's Maria and Sylvie—oh, hell. Come and talk to Maria. I can't explain."

They walked into the kitchen together. Maria looked up. "You found her," she said.

Rhea's mother nodded. Her lips were tight and bloodless.

The cook reached over and laid her hand on Rhea's mother's fingers, where they dug into the back of a chair. *"It will be all right,"* she said.

Perhaps there was a little magic in it. Rhea was never sure if Maria had been telling all the truth about all her magic being taken away. Regardless, her mother exhaled, long and slow, and stood a little straighter.

"You found her," said Maria again.

"*How* did you find me?" asked Rhea. It occurred to her suddenly that if her mother was in the house, her father might be, too—and the priest and the viscount and all the members of the wedding party. They would probably avoid the kitchen, but still . . .

Perhaps she had been in the house too long, with too few souls. The notion of other people filled her with sudden gray panic.

What if they see what's happening? They can't help. They'll make it worse. It could be so much worse. If my parents are here—oh, no! What if Aunt's here? She'll be all over the place looking for dust!

"Where's Aunt?" she asked sharply.

"Minding the mill," said her mother dryly. "She was extremely upset not to be invited, but we convinced her that we'd lose money if she wasn't there to take the grain orders."

Rhea's panic gave way to relief.

Crevan probably didn't pay her a thought. He has my parents, why would it matter if he threatened my aunt, too?

I suppose if we all die, she might be able to convince Skeller that something rotten has happened. Or maybe he'll turn her out because the whole thing is so unpleasant and he doesn't want to deal with it.

Still, the fact that she did not have to deal with her aunt's prying questions was a kindness in a day that promised to have few kindnesses to offer.

"Are the other guests . . . ?" Rhea peered out the doorway.

"The mother of the bride is allowed to wander the house, looking for her daughter," said Maria firmly. "The other guests are in the courtyard. That's where Ingeth has been setting out the food." She nodded to Rhea's mother. "Will you be a dear and go see if you can find Ingeth?

* * *

A tall woman, with a scarred throat. Tell her we need the dress brought down. It's almost time."

"It can't be almost time," said Rhea once her mother had gone. Her face felt sticky, and her hair was limp. "I don't . . . I'm not . . . I can't get married like *this*!"

Maria sighed. "Does it matter?"

(It was embarrassing to admit that it did. Rhea felt that she *should* have been willing to be dragged to the altar in chains, with her hair in snarls, and yet the thought of being ragged and dirty and humiliated, in addition to being trapped, was infuriating.)

"Why do we always want to dress up for the gallows?" asked Maria. "Never mind, child—that was rhetorical."

"He'll get mad if I look like a beggar," said Rhea. "It'll embarrass him in front of all his grand friends."

"Not so many grand friends," said Maria. "There's only the viscount and one or two of his hangers-on—and they don't look any too comfortable. Himself is not as popular with the gentry as he'd like to be, I think."

Rhea scowled. "Can't he . . . I don't know . . . get a charming wife and take the charm off her?"

I am joking about this. I am actually joking. Oh, Lady of Stones, I've gone mad and out the other side again . . .

Maria snorted. "If we fail, I'll suggest it, shall I?"

"Ha," said Rhea.

Maria moved suddenly, locking her arms around Rhea in a bear hug. Rhea started to squirm involuntarily, then realized what was happening.

"You are strong," said Maria quietly. "If you fail, it won't be for lack of trying. And if you fail, I won't forget you. A witch's memory is worth something, even if I'm hardly a witch at all anymore."

She let go. Rhea blinked, feeling touched (and a little squashed) and not entirely sure if she had been honored or cursed.

"Here's a comb," said Maria briskly. "Wash your face in the scullery and get the knots out. You ought to have your hair up like a proper bride, but we'll make do."

And like that, the moment passed. Rhea went into the scullery, ran a little fresh water, and scrubbed her face. She would not be beautiful, but she could at least be clean.

"This is not how I pictured your wedding day," said her mother from the door. She held the red dress a little away from her body, as if it might bite. "I thought—well—I suppose it doesn't matter."

Her mother's grief was such a small sin to put on the ledger alongside Sylvie and the golem wife and her own very probable death, and yet Rhea took note of it anyway. She would make Crevan pay for his crimes—or she would die, and someone else would come along, and she would be remembered only by her parents and by a woman who was no longer a witch.

Well.

Either way.

"I would probably still have gotten dressed in the kitchen," Rhea said. She dredged up a smile from somewhere. It felt strange on her face. "And I'd rather have Maria here than Aunt anyway."

She put her arm around her mother and noticed for the first time how thin her mother seemed, how fine and fragile her bones.

She hoped that, if she died in the clock, she would simply vanish and her mother might think that she had managed to run away. If not . . . well . . . if her gear-mangled body was spat out onto the tiles, she hoped someone would have the sense to keep her mother from seeing it.

And if I do vanish, and they think I've run, will Crevan take it out on you as well?

She was terribly afraid that he would. Perhaps she was dooming her family to homelessness and ruin, no matter what she did.

She could not even warn her mother, for fear that he was listening. "To hell with the mill," her mother had said.

I hope you meant that, Mother. Because I can't let him keep doing this. I have to try, whatever the cost.

She squeezed her mother's shoulders once, hard, wishing that she could push the knowledge of what she was trying to do through the skin between them.

Her mother squeezed back.

Rhea took a deep breath. "Well," she said. "I suppose it's time to dress."

There were no mirrors in the kitchen, but Rhea could tell by Maria's expression that the dress was not an unmitigated success.

"You look lovely," said her mother, but she sounded more like a woman at a funeral than at a wedding.

"Indeed," said a deep voice from the door. "Lovely."

All three of them looked up toward Lord Crevan, and only Maria did not flinch.

"Miss Rhea," he said. And to her mother, "Madam."

Her mother curtseyed. She cast Rhea a frightened glance, but Rhea could not make her knees bend.

If I try in this dress, I'll probably pop out all the stitches . . .

"Milord," she said.

"I came to make sure that there were no difficulties," he said.

There were a dozen things that Rhea could have said. She said none of them, because her mother was in the room.

He probably wouldn't care if she saw me insult him. He probably would think nothing of it. But if he did . . .

And even if he didn't care, it would only upset Mother.

"I'm sure it will be fine, milord," said Rhea quietly.

He smiled. "I have guests to attend to," he said. "As I'd hoped, the viscount has done me the honor of attending. I shall send Ingeth when we are ready."

Rhea nodded.

He went away again. The sound of his boot heels on the tiles clicked into the distance.

Rhea's mother let out her breath slowly. "He does not act like a man about to be wed," she said.

Maria caught Rhea's eye. "Yes, well. These things take people differently. Will you go out, ma'am, and come tell us when it is nearly time? I don't think these stitches will hold for much longer, and if she needs to sit down, I'll want to let out the hips."

Rhea's mother nodded and went out. Maria reached down under the table and plopped the hedgehog in front of Rhea. "You've been poking me in the ankle for the last ten minutes," she said. "Once would have been enough. I'm not so dense as all that."

The hedgehog looked unrepentant.

"I've sewn you a pocket for stray hedgehogs," said Maria. "It's in the left sleeve. And take your knife."

Rhea tucked both knife and hedgehog into their respective positions. Her sleeves felt unexpectedly heavy, but it was a reassuring weight.

"Hopefully there's nothing you'll have to stab," said Maria briskly. "But better safe than sorry."

Rhea drank another cup of tea. Her hands were shaking, but the weight of the mug helped steady them. She could not hear the clock ticking from the next room, but she thought she could feel it in her fingertips and her jaw and the small bones of her ears.

Nerves. It's nerves.

Lots of brides are nervous, she thought, and had to put her forehead down on the table for a minute to stifle hysterical laughter. Maria gave her a level look, but did not comment.

Her mother did not return. Instead Ingeth came, and glared at them both. She made a brisk beckoning gesture to Rhea.

"Time, then," said Maria. "Go on ahead, Ingeth. We're coming."

Ingeth shook her head and reached for Rhea's wrist.

Maria, moving with startling speed, knocked the hand away. "You will not manhandle the bride on her wedding day," she said icily. "She'll get plenty of that from Himself. I *said* we're coming."

Ingeth tried to stare down Maria, failed miserably, and then looked away as if she hadn't been trying. She shook her head, pressed her lips together, and stalked away.

"She suspects," said Maria. "Doesn't surprise me, given everything she's overheard in the past week. Whether she'll try to stop us, I don't know. We have to go now."

"I wanted to say good-bye to my mother one last time," said Rhea softly. "But there's no time, is there? I have to go now, before the ceremony."

Maria sighed and took her arm. They walked across the tile floor together. "You'll have plenty of time inside," she murmured. "For all the good it does. Try not to die of old age."

"That could happen?"

"It's a clock, child."

They stopped in front of the clock case. Rhea licked her dry lips.

Maria put her hand on the case and murmured a word.

The clock opened.

"I thought you didn't have any magic left," said Rhea, feeling unexpectedly betrayed.

"I might have exaggerated a bit," said Maria with a shrug.

Rhea stared into the clock. A pendulum swung back and forth. Gears ground together. How was she supposed to fit inside?

The hedgehog squirmed in her pocket. She pulled it out and set it down on the ground.

It trudged resolutely forward, into the clock, and vanished under the pendulum. Was there a point of entry there?

Rhea knelt down. The dress's seams groaned and a hasty stitch popped.

There looked to be a passage—a very small one, barely big enough for her head, never mind her shoulders—

"Go!" hissed Maria. "I'll hold the way open, but you have to go. I don't trust Ingeth."

"But I can't fit—" began Rhea.

Maria put one foot squarely on her red-clad backside and shoved.

Rhea fell out of the world and into the clock.

Chapter Twenty-Five

It was dark. Then it wasn't.

Rhea crawled forward on her knees and forearms through what felt like a dark tunnel, feeling the weight of metal mechanisms over her head—and then there was light, and she was not in a tunnel at all.

She was on a vast plain covered in checkerboard tiles.

She stood up, rubbing her rear end where Maria had shoved her. She was a bit annoyed about that, but this did not seem like the time to dwell on it.

The plain seemed to stretch in all directions. If she had come from a tunnel, it had vanished. The light streamed down from overhead, a dull, directionless illumination.

Whatever Rhea had expected, it wasn't this.

"Hello?" she called. "Hello?"

Should I call out her name? What is her name? I can't just call her Clock Wife, can I?

Sure. Then she can call me Girl Wife. This'll work out well.

"Hello?" she tried again.

She looked around for the hedgehog, but it was nowhere in sight.

Well, the tile floor is the same as the one in the manor house . . .

For lack of anything better to do, she set out briskly in no particular direction.

At least I can avoid going in circles . . .

By keeping her feet firmly on one line of tile, she could be sure that she was going straight ahead and not wandering off in any direction.

Which is useful. I guess?

She walked for a few minutes and then stopped because staring at the horizon was making her eyes cross. She was starting to wish that the tiled floor in the manor house had been something other than checkerboard. Perhaps a nice solid terra-cotta. Something that didn't seem to jitter and wiggle off on the horizon.

Though she could see a great distance—or what she thought to be a great distance—she could not see the hedgehog anywhere.

I hope it's okay . . .

The world went *bonnnggg.*

It was the crashing, grinding noise of the floor falling, magnified ten thousand times. The bones in her ears thrummed, and her rib cage seemed to flex in on itself, unable to absorb the noise. Her heart pounded against the sound, each beat feeling sticky, as if it were trapped in a wall of glue.

Rhea dropped to the ground and curled up in a ball like she'd seen the hedgehog do so many times, trying to fit herself onto a single tile. Another seam in her dress popped.

If this tile falls, I'll fall with it, what do I do, can I ride it down, oh god, oh god, it's so loud!

But the tile she was on shot upward.

She had an instant to think, *Wait, this is backward,* and then she was soaring into the sky.

The force of the rushing air pinned her to the tile, which was good. She found an edge with her hand and curled her fingers around it. If the tile fitted against others, somewhere up above, she might get her fingers crushed, but if she fell, she would lose a lot more than fingers.

She could not see because the wind made her eyes tear up, and even though she thought she was screaming, she could not hear through the sound of the clock.

Oh, please let the hedgehog have gotten away. It couldn't survive something like this on its own. It would get blown off—crushed—please let it be somewhere else.

She clung to the tile, and eventually she stopped screaming, because it didn't seem to be helping. The wind blew against her face, and her fingers were so cold she could hardly feel them anymore.

She did not sleep—sleep would have been impossible, not to mention insane—but she went away in her head to a place that was a little like sleep. She did not think, she did not act, she lay on the tile with the wind hammering against her while fragments of images danced in her head, one step short of dreams.

A long time later, or what felt like a long time later, the wind seemed to slacken. She opened her eyes.

She was sitting on the edge of a beach. The tile underneath her was obscured by small black pebbles. The wind that blew in from the water smelled of salt and ice and cold.

Rhea took a deep breath, sobbed once, and then shoved the rest down. She had no time—or she had plenty of time, she wasn't sure. She stood.

It was strangely quiet and strangely loud, all at the same time. The water slopped against the beach, an endless over and under of sound, and yet the whole place seemed awash with silence. The din of the waves muffled out any other sound. She had never seen anything like it, because in her whole life, Rhea had never seen the sea.

She stared at it for a few moments, transfixed, and then dragged her eyes away. *It's like staring into the fire. Always moving, always changing, and hours could go by before you notice . . .*

The sky overhead was white with clouds. The water was gray. The small black stones slid underfoot.

As she turned to gain her bearings, she felt her feet slide in opposite directions.

Ice hung over her.

It was a mountain of ice, a shattered cathedral of ice, pressed into fantastic blue-green shapes. It leaned out over the beach and arched over Rhea's head.

Rhea's mind skittered frantically and landed on the word *glacier*.

She scrambled backward, practically falling, trying to get out from under the leaning wall. It looked as if it would collapse at any instant and bury her under unknown tons of ice.

But it did not fall.

She finally tripped over her own feet and fell backward, with the shadow of the glacier just touching her skirts. Her breath whooshed out, and she panted, staring up at the ice wall . . . and still it did not fall.

Gradually her breathing slowed. She got to her feet and thought, *I am running away from ice. What do I expect it to do, bite me?*

Why is there a glacier and a beach inside the clock?

She shoved stray bits of hair out of her face and stared up at the ice. *Oh*. Oh. *Maria said the clock wife was from up north. And Sylvie said there were things in the ice . . .*

"This is where she's staying," said a voice just over her left shoulder.

Rhea whirled.

Sylvie was standing behind her.

It took Rhea a moment to recognize her. She was not wearing a bandage. This Sylvie had clear gray eyes and gazed at Rhea. When Rhea shifted on her feet, Sylvie's eyes moved to follow.

She can see. She isn't blind.

"Sylvie?" asked Rhea. Her voice cracked a little. "What are you doing in here?"

"Do I know you?" Sylvie tilted her head. "Did Maria put you in the clock, too?"

The words slipped into Rhea's mind like a dagger slipping between her ribs.

Did Maria put you in the clock, too?

Too?

Rhea swallowed hard.

"Yes . . . ?"

Sylvie nodded.

There was still no sound on the beach but the slopping of water against the shore. Rhea wrapped her arms around herself to keep out the cold. The stupid red dress flapped around her knees.

Sylvie was wearing a white dress. Combined with her white skin and white hair, she looked as colorless as the sky.

"Did she . . . did you . . . ?" Rhea made a useless little gesture with one hand and felt desperately foolish.

"Yes," said Sylvie. "I couldn't find her, so I went out again." She lowered her head, gazing at the ground. "Most of me did. I'm still here. But I'm out there, too."

The words chased each other around in Rhea's head, and she struggled to catch them and string them together in a way that made any sort of sense.

She went into the clock and went out again—and she's not blind here and—

Oh, Lady of Stones.

Had Maria put Sylvie into the clock *before* she'd gone blind? On her own wedding day perhaps?

Had she already tried to wake the clock wife?

But she came out—but she's still here*!*

"How is that possible?"

"Ask Maria."

Sylvie didn't sound angry, Rhea noted. She sounded rather distant and matter-of-fact about it.

Time is strange in the clock, Maria warned me, but she didn't warn me that I wasn't the first!

Had Sylvie tried to warn her? She had said that Maria could be ruthless. Was this what she had meant?

If Sylvie failed—but of course she failed, she's been married to Crevan for years—

Oh, Lady of Stones, how many other wives have tried this? Has she been throwing us all into the clock in the hopes that one of us will succeed?

Maria, what have you been you doing?

And then another thought, like a sliver of ice working inward— *Does she actually hope that one of us will succeed?*

What if she's putting us in the clock for some reason of her own? What if this has nothing to do with waking the clock wife at all, and she's stuffing us in here so that . . . so that . . .

Rhea's imagination failed her. If Maria had some other reason to trap the other wives in the clock, she could not think of it. *Is it a witch thing? Does she have some kind of plan that will get her free? Is it some magic with the clock?*

Was Maria really waiting for her outside the clock?

Well. If it was magic, there was no telling. Rhea's experience with magic had not included explanations.

Pebbles rattled against each other as Sylvie crouched down on the shore.

"Have you been here long?" asked Rhea. She thought that her voice sounded remarkably steady, given the circumstances.

I am not curling into a little ball and screaming. I wish someone else were here to be impressed by how much I am not screaming right now.

Sylvie looked up at that. "I don't know," she said. "I went out just a little while ago, didn't I? The rest of me? We must have met then, because I don't remember you."

"Yes," said Rhea. "Yes, we met then. It's—ah—it's been a little while since you left."

"Oh," said Sylvie. She looked out over the water, which was the same color as her eyes. "Maria said time might be strange here. Are my parents well?"

"So far as I know . . ." Rhea racked her brain for anything that Sylvie—*her* Sylvie—might have said about her parents and could only remember her saying not to judge them too harshly. "I haven't heard anything bad."

"That's all right, then," said Sylvie.

She said nothing more for a few moments, which was long enough for Rhea to think of a great many frightening things. *If time is strange here, and Sylvie thinks she just left, then how long have I really been in here? What if I was riding the tile for hours, weeks, years? What if everyone has died of old age out there?*

Then Crevan will be dead, too, she thought tartly, *and my biggest problem will have been solved.*

Sylvie looked away from the water and smiled at her—a familiar, slightly worried, slightly confused smile. "I'm sorry, have we met?"

"Just now . . . ," said Rhea.

"Oh. Did Maria put you in the clock, too?"

Rhea inhaled sharply.

This Sylvie is not *all here. The one outside isn't, either, but . . .*

If I get out of the clock, will I leave something inside that thinks it's me? Will I go back and be sort of vague and silly and easily distracted?

Is that what Maria wants?

Rhea took a deep breath. *I suppose I'll worry about that if I ever manage to get out. If Maria's betrayed me, there's nothing I can do. I guess I just keep going.*

"She did. I'm supposed to let the clock wife out," Rhea said cautiously. "Can you help me?"

"She's in there," said Sylvie, pointing to the glacier. "I found her eventually. She's very angry, and she shakes the clock. Most of the time, though, she just wants to curl up in there."

"Can you show me?" asked Rhea.

Sylvie nodded.

They picked their way across the stones, moving parallel to the glacier. "Down here," said Sylvie, pointing ahead. "It goes a long way, but she's not far. The ice sticks out, and it meets the water in the inlet, and she's inside."

"Not far" seemed to be about half a mile, which would have been easier if the beach had not been strewn with sliding, ankle-turning stones. Sylvie forgot Rhea twice as they walked and had to be reminded again, and then reassured that her parents were well.

I hope she remembers where we're going. I wonder how many times I'll have to introduce myself before it sticks.

A long finger of land stuck out, away from the glacier, and they turned to cross it, putting the sea at their backs. Rhea was glad to leave the strangely moving water. It seemed to her that Sylvie was more forgetful when she was looking at the waves.

The rocks underfoot grew larger until they were nearly the size of Rhea's fist. She had to work her way carefully across them, and they jabbed through the thin soles of her shoes as she walked.

"There," Sylvie said and pointed.

Rhea looked up.

The glacier reared in front of them. It was a deep green color, utterly unlike anything Rhea had ever seen in nature. There were no flowers that color, no leaves, nothing she recognized at all.

From where they stood, the sea streamed in on the right, forming a shallow inlet. The glacier met the sea and ended in a rounded nub, polished by waves. The pool at the base was cloudy white, like milk.

"In there?" said Rhea.

Sylvie nodded.

Rhea stared at the uncompromising ice.

"What am I supposed to do now?" she said aloud. "Build a fire and melt her out?"

She glanced up and down the beach. There was nothing to burn—only those endless black rocks and pebbles.

How do I even know she's in there? Sylvie could be completely wrong, or have forgotten.

And then she heard it—so faint that she could hardly be sure it was there, so faint that it might have been wishful thinking.

Tapping.

The same tapping she had heard from the clock, the tapping that she had followed through the house.

Rhea took a step forward, straining her ears over the sound of the waves.

There it was again—tap, tap, tap.

Something's in there.

Sylvie's gaze strayed toward the water. Rhea cleared her throat loudly, and the woman who was not blind here looked back at her. "Yes?"

"How do I get her to let me in?" asked Rhea, clinging to the last shreds of her patience.

Sylvie shook her head. "I haven't figured that out," she said. "I don't think . . . unless I forgot . . ." Her gaze grew unfocused again.

Great. If I leave part of me in the clock, apparently that chunk will lose its memory. My memory. This gets better and better all the time.

She wondered again how much time had passed. It didn't feel like that long.

Apparently it doesn't feel like that long to Sylvie, either.

There was a large stone on the beach that stuck a little way into the milky-white pool. Rhea stepped out onto it and reached a hand up to the slick knob of the glacier.

It was very cold.

Well, what did I expect?

"Let me in," she said hopelessly. "Let me in, Clock Wife, if you can hear me. It's me, Rhea. I slept against you all this week. I don't know if you remember . . ."

And then, because she could not think of anything else to do, she balled her hand into a fist and knocked on the ice like it was a door.

The return knock was so immediate that it startled her. She jerked backward, windmilling her arms to keep from falling into the water. Hypothermia might not be real in the clock, but she didn't want to take a chance.

The knock sounded like someone tapping on the other side of a door. Rhea lifted her hand and tapped again.

Was it an echo? It didn't sound like an echo . . .

The knock was returned, first one soft tap, then two.

Rhea tapped twice.

A flurry of pounding came from behind the ice, so loud and sudden that she retreated back from the glacier, her eyes wide.

Clearly it was not an echo.

"When someone knocks," said Sylvie, "you should let them in. As long as it's before dark."

"What if it's after dark?" asked Rhea. She glanced up at the sky, which was still the same pale gray it had been when she arrived.

Sylvie considered this. "They might be monsters, then," she said. "Things melted out of the glacier . . ."

"I'm pretty sure that's exactly what she is," said Rhea, fighting an urge to laugh hysterically. "Let her *in*? How do I let her *out*?"

Another knock, tentative. Was the clock wife afraid she had left?

She squared her shoulders and knocked back. "I'm still here," she said, putting her face so close to the ice that she could feel cold air against her lips. "I can't open the ice. You'll have to open it. Please come out, or let me in, or just open the door."

Silence.

Rhea let out a long sigh and saw her breath melt a tiny slickness on the ice.

The wall cracked.

It made a sound like a door slamming closed—or open. A lightning-bolt crack spread across the surface, splitting into a hundred separate cracks as it went.

Rhea retreated to the beach. Bits of opaque green ice shattered off the end of the glacier, pattering into the water. The white pool frothed.

The large crack—the one she'd been watching—split open. The interior was not dark, but lit with a crazy quilt of reflections, as light struck the faceted ice and bounced off it.

Curled up inside, her knees drawn to her chest, lay the clock wife.

Chapter Twenty-Six

If Rhea had thought about it at all, she would have expected the clock wife to be pale the way that Sylvie was pale, a creature of the northern ice and pale northern sun.

But she was not. Her skin was dark blue-gray, the color of flint, a color found on no human being that Rhea had ever met. When she opened her eyes, they were the shocking green color of glacial ice.

The clock wife lifted her head and stared directly at Rhea.

Rhea said, "Hello?"

"You have knocked," said the clock wife. Her voice was deep and resonant, like the clock's chimes. "It was you."

"It was," said Rhea. She could not tell if the clock wife was angry or pleased or if she felt anything at all. Her face was finely carved and expressionless.

The flint-skinned woman unfolded herself from the ice and stood up. She left a neat hole behind her, like the hollow left by a peach pit.

She towered over Rhea. Rhea took a step back. *Was she that tall before? Did she just curl up very tight in there, or is she growing?*

The clock wife caught her arm.

Rhea had expected that the other woman's touch would be cold, like the ice, but it was burning hot. Gray fingers lay across Rhea's wrist, making her brown skin look as blazing red as the wedding dress by contrast.

"This is still the clock," said the clock wife. "I was in the ice, and then I was called out. Then I was shut into the clock. I went back into the ice and waited to be called out. But you have called me out, and *this is still the clock.*"

Her grip tightened as she spoke, until Rhea could not hold back a gasp. She could feel the bones in her wrist creaking.

She looked around for Sylvie, but the other woman was already wandering down the beach, gazing at the water. There was no help from her.

The clock wife gripped harder.

"I'm trying to get you out of the clock," Rhea said. "I'm in the clock with you. My friend is going to get us both out if she can. Please, you're hurting me!"

The clock wife's impassive green eyes bored into her, and then the cruel grip released.

"This is not how it was," said the clock wife. "You are not who came to me before. That was another one, and I now do not love him. This is a new happening, not the one before?"

"Yes?" said Rhea, cradling her arm.

The clock wife nodded. "Very well."

She stepped away and scanned the beach. Rhea swallowed a few times.

What do I do now? I thought if I found her, I could tell her what I needed, but she seems even more confused than Sylvie in some ways . . .

The clock wife bent down and picked up a stone. She turned it over in her hands, as if it were the most fascinating thing in the world.

"I need your help," said Rhea.

"Now?" said the clock wife.

"Errr . . . yes? Or soon anyway." Rhea licked her lips, trying to decide how to continue. "I'm supposed to marry Lord Crevan—"

"Him!" said the clock wife, and the stone was crushed to powder in her hands and sifted down between her fingers. "He called me from the ice. I was grateful then, but the one who is *I* now is not grateful. I would go and tell the one who called herself *I* then, but there is no changing the past except by reliving it."

Rhea had to stop and work that one out in her head. "Errr. Yes. Well, he's out there now. Outside the clock."

"Yesss . . ." The clock wife made a stroking hiss of the word. "Yes, he is. I can smell him in the air around the clock. I have tried to pull the world away from him, but the clock prevents me. There is only one gap, but no matter how often I relive it, I cannot get to him."

Is she . . . is she talking about making the floor fall?

One gap . . . Does she think she's only done it once? Has she just been reliving the same moment over and over, trying to get to him?

Maria said time was strange in the clock, but this is making my head ache.

"I want to help you get to him," said Rhea cautiously. "If I can."

"To do that, I now must leave the clock." She dusted sand from her hands. "Perhaps I should go back in the ice and wait again . . ."

"No!" said Rhea. "That won't help. My friend can get us out of the clock—I think—but you will have to come out and face Crevan if you do."

"Crevan?" said Sylvie, looking up. She had been watching the tide and had come slowly back up the beach. "Is he here?"

"I will unmake him," said the clock wife simply. "I will pull the marrow from his bones and pour lead into the spaces left behind. I will make his dying into a place and visit it every day until the end of eternity. But he is not *here*."

"I don't think he's all *that* bad," said Sylvie doubtfully. "My parents liked him."

"He has taken my death," said the clock wife grimly. "My death, which walked with me from the moment I was born. He wed me and took my death as a wedding gift unasked. I do not forgive. I then was foolish with gratitude for leaving the ice. I now do not make this mistake again."

Sylvie's eyes were round at this. She looked at Rhea. "Did you understand that?"

"I understood well enough," said Rhea. She squared her shoulders. "If you come out of the clock and help me, we'll . . . we'll try and get your death back."

"I now do not ask this," said the clock wife, folding her arms over her breast. "My death is gone. It became someone else's death. I now am no monster, to take it back from one who it has loved. A poor gift that would be, for an old friend."

Rhea took a deep breath. "Will you help me anyway?"

"You ask?" said the clock wife.

Rhea nodded. "Please. He's going to marry me and do something terrible to me. I need your help to stop him."

The clock wife rubbed her hands through her hair. It was very short, Rhea noticed, and it rippled strangely under her fingers, like a cat's pelt.

"He would not take your death," murmured the clock wife. "Your past is short. The one who was you has barely stepped aside from the one who *is* you. That is what he would take, that shortness. You understand?"

Rhea shook her head hopelessly. "I'm sorry. I don't."

The clock wife folded her hands together, fingertips touching her lips. Her expression was one of fierce concentration.

She's trying . . . I think she's really trying. I think it's hard for her. Maybe she's not confused like Sylvie. Maybe it's just really hard for her to talk to people who can't relive time. I now, I then . . . those words must mean more to her than they do to me.

"Time," said the clock wife. "Not the place. The happening of it. That is it. Yours. He will take the days of your life to come so he lives them instead, and you will have nothing to relive. He has drunk too much of his time, so he seeks to pour more days into his cup. You understand?"

Rhea nodded.

Youth. That's what she's talking about. He's going to take my youth to make himself younger, like Maria suspected. That's why he wanted to marry me so young. It's a gift he would like to keep for himself.

Well. Well. It was what she had been gnawing over for a week. Hearing the clock wife confirm it should not have felt so much like a blow to the chest. *I suppose . . . I suppose it could be worse, right?* She stifled a hysterical laugh. It was better than what he had done to the golem wife. Even if Crevan drank down all her years and left her nothing but bones and dust, it was still better than that.

The clock wife shook her head slowly. "Help," she said. "My help. I now could. I then would have. I now am not I then. So close to a reliving, this place. To come out of the ice to a wedding." She narrowed her glass-green eyes. "How do I now know that you do not mean betrayal?"

"You just said he was going to take my youth," said Rhea. "Isn't that proof that I'm not on his side?"

"You might be a fool," said the clock wife. "There are many and will be many more who serve those who will be harming them."

"I hope I'm not a fool," said Rhea, raking her fingers through her hair. She laughed. *Except for the bit where you let Maria put you in the clock, without her mentioning that she'd done it before.* "Or if it's too late for that, I hope I'm at least not *that* kind of fool."

The clock wife said nothing.

"Here," said Rhea, thrusting out her hand. The engagement ring was as cold a gray as the clock wife's skin. "Here's the ring. He means to marry me."

The clock wife took Rhea's hand. She was careful this time, holding it very delicately, and yet Rhea could still feel the inhuman heat of that grip.

"Yesss . . ."

She held out her own hand. It took a moment for Rhea to distinguish gray metal on gray skin, but there it was, unmistakable.

"You, too," said Rhea.

"I, too. I now, I then. Yesss."

Rhea rubbed her hands together, feeling her fingertips skid over the ring.

"Give me a death," said the clock wife. "Your days for an end to mine. That is what I now ask. That is the price for help."

A death? Does she want me to kill her? Or—no, if she's taking my death, does that mean I'll die? Or that I won't ever die?

I should probably be really worried about immortality and maybe my soul or something, but I don't have time for this!

"All right," said Rhea. "After Crevan's . . . dealt with. You can have mine, if another one doesn't come along."

"What do you now swear by?" asked the clock wife, cocking her head. It was a birdlike movement, deeply alien.

"By the Lady of Stones," said Rhea.

"It is well. It will be well. I now swear by the past uneaten and the Mother Unending. Is it well?"

"It is well."

"Then let us now go."

Chapter Twenty-Seven

The clock wife looked at her expectantly. Rhea rubbed her sweaty palms on the sides of her dress. "Ah. Yes. Do you know how to get out?"

"If I then knew how to get out, I now would not be here."

I thought she'd know how to get out. Or at least have some idea. Or Maria would be watching somehow, and she'd get us out.

Assuming I can even trust Maria not to leave half of me inside the clock . . .

This was not helpful.

It's all right. I've gotten this far. I'll work it out on my own.

"Um. Just a minute . . . ," she said to the clock wife.

Rhea hurried over to Sylvie, who was gazing over the water with a faint smile on her lips. "Sylvie."

The pale woman turned. "Oh. Hello. Do I know you?"

I am not going to scream. I'm not. I've gotten the clock wife to agree to help me, and now I just need to figure out how to get us out of here.

"No," said Rhea. "You've never met me. Maria told me to find you."

"Oh! How is Maria? Did she put you in—"

"The clock, yes. Listen very carefully, Sylvie. I need your help."

Sylvie leaned forward. "Of course. What can I do?"

It's a good thing you're basically so nice. This would be a lot harder if it was Ingeth in here . . .

"When you left the clock before," said Rhea. "The part of you that left. Where did it go?"

"Oh," said Sylvie. "Out through the clock again. I can show you, but that way has been closed for . . . oh, a little while, I think. I'm not sure how long."

"Can you take me there?"

"Sure," Sylvie said and began to pick her way along the curve of the beach, away from the bulk of the glacier.

Rhea hurried after her. The clock wife followed, taking one stride for every three of Rhea's.

"My village is this way," said Sylvie. "Well, it's sort of my village. There's nobody there. It's sad. I don't go there often, I don't think— although I was just there, wasn't I?" She shook herself. "Anyway, there's a clock in my house. There wasn't one in the real house, so I don't think it's quite a real clock, do you?"

"That seems likely," said Rhea.

"I thought so."

It did not take very long to reach the village. Rhea wasn't sure if Sylvie had actually lived in the shadow of the glacier or if everything was skewed because they were inside the clock.

The real Sylvie talked about things melting out of the glacier in summer and coming up at night, so I suppose the village might have been close by . . .

As they left the beach behind and struck inland, the stones gave way to earth. Rhea sighed with relief. Her aching feet did better on the even ground than they had on the shifting beach.

The clock wife appeared to be barefoot. Perhaps when you were not human and not entirely tethered in time, little inconveniences like rocks didn't bother you.

Grass covered the earth, spangled with tiny flowers. There were even a few low bushes and some sort of heather. And then, quite suddenly, they were standing in the middle of the village.

It was an odd little place. They were already among the houses before Rhea even realized that the shapes were man-made. The houses were made of some low, shaggy material—sod, maybe? Was it sod that made the houses look hairy? The roofs were covered in grass. The doors were made of wood, and the few windows were tightly shuttered.

"In here," said Sylvie, heading to one of the houses and pulling open the door. "Watch your step."

Rhea followed her, stepping down and down again. To her surprise, the house was actually quite large, with an unexpectedly high ceiling—it was merely recessed deep into the earth. Even the clock wife, following her down the steps, did not need to duck her head.

"Here it is," said Sylvie, sounding exasperated. "Foolish thing. Anyway, it doesn't work."

Rhea's eyebrows climbed.

The clock was identical to the one in Crevan's manor. It stood directly in the middle of the floor, where it would present the maximum amount of inconvenience to anyone trying to live in the house. Rhea couldn't imagine any human willingly putting it there. For one thing, the back corner was actually *in* the fireplace.

Unlike the one in the manor clock, this clock's pendulum hung still and silent. Rhea opened the glass and pushed the pendulum with her finger. It ticked a few times, halfheartedly, then fell silent.

"It is dead," said the clock wife. "If it was a passage then, it is not a passage now."

"I went through it," said Sylvie. "The rest of me. Except *I* didn't."

"Maria's supposed to help us through," muttered Rhea. "Maria?" She leaned into the clock's mechanism and called out the cook's name, feeling vaguely foolish. "Maria? Are you there?"

There was no answer.

Rhea felt panic start to rise in her belly and squelched it. *Maybe she was called away. Maybe she'll be back.*

Maybe I'm yelling into the wrong clock.

"Are there any other strange clocks around?" she asked.

Sylvie looked puzzled. "Isn't one enough?"

"Apparently not!" Rhea slapped the case shut with the flat of her hand. "I can't go through this one!"

"Well, it's not your clock," said Sylvie reasonably. "Maybe it was my clock. It's in *my* house . . ."

"You mean there's a clock in *my* house?" asked Rhea. "But is my house even here?"

"Time is a large country," observed the clock wife.

"Great," muttered Rhea. "So if we're in Sylvie's house now, then my house should be, what, a thousand miles south and a bit east?"

The notion of traveling all that way made her feel physically queasy. *I know time doesn't pass the same way in here, but surely I'm not meant to walk the length of a continent. Besides, magic or not, how would we walk over water?*

She leaned her forehead on the clock case. The glass felt cold against her skin.

Well. Now what?

I could check all the other houses for clocks, I suppose . . . or maybe the clock wife will have some idea, if I can figure out what she's saying . . .

Something bumped her foot.

She opened her eyes and looked down, and there was the hedgehog.

"Oh, thank the Lady," she said, her voice cracking. "I was afraid you'd gotten lost."

The hedgehog gave her one of its familiar looks.

"I know, I know. I'm loster than you. More lost. You know." Rhea rubbed her hand over her face.

"A hedgehog!" said Sylvie. "How darling!"

Rhea waited, but apparently the clock wife had no opinion on hedgehogs at this time.

"Do you know the way out?" asked Rhea, crouching down. "You're good at that."

It tapped her shoe and turned away. Rhea rose and followed.

There was a hatch set in the floor of the house. "It's the root cellar," said Sylvie. And then, doubtfully, "I don't *think* there's a clock in there . . ."

The hedgehog poked its snout at the hatch and looked up at Rhea.

"If it says this is the way, then it's the way," said Rhea firmly. "I would follow this hedgehog into the mouth of hell."

The hedgehog looked pleased by this. Rhea pulled the hatch open—there was an iron ring set in it—and peered down the stairs into the darkness.

"This way?"

A nod. It stepped onto her hand and suffered itself to be placed into its pocket.

Rhea descended the steps.

It was dark, and it only got darker. The square of light from the hatch was blocked by Sylvie, and then by the clock wife. In that faint illumination, she found their hands—one soft and cool, one almost scalding.

Hand in hand, the three walked into the darkness.

For the first time since she had entered the clock, Rhea felt confident. This was correct. Perhaps she did not need a clock. Perhaps all she had needed was darkness.

Perhaps magic had to happen in the dark.

"Maria?" she called. "Maria, can you hear me?"

She could feel her companions' footsteps through their hands—Sylvie's careful, the clock wife's slow and sure.

The hedgehog shifted in her pocket, leaning left. Rhea took it as a cue and angled that way as well. The light from the hatch vanished behind them.

"I don't remember the root cellar being this big," said Sylvie doubtfully. "We should have run into shelves and things by now."

"I don't think we're in the root cellar," said Rhea.

The hedgehog leaned again. Rhea shifted to follow.

She did not know how long they walked through the darkness inside the clock, but they seemed to be angling downward. *I went up a long way on the tile. Maybe I have to go back down . . .*

Finally the hedgehog leaned back. Spines prickled her skin through the pocket, and Rhea stopped.

"Here?" she asked.

A very small shrug was her answer. Rhea cleared her throat. "Maria? Maria, can you hear—"

A door opened, and light poured into the darkness. Through it, Rhea could see checkerboard tiles and Maria's face.

Clutching her companions' hands, burning herself on the clock wife's skin, Rhea fell forward, out of the clock, and into Maria's arms.

Chapter Twenty-Eight

"I brought her," she said, hearing her own voice high and babbling in her ears. "I brought her, Maria. She said she'll help, but she wants a death, that's all, somebody's death. I don't know what it means, but I said she could have mine . . ."

She turned her head, and the clock wife came stepping out of the clock like a woman emerging from water. Her hand in Rhea's was suddenly fiery, and Rhea had to jerk her fingers away.

Maria set Rhea on her feet and bowed deeply to the clock wife.

"Witch," said the clock wife, inclining her head.

"Power," said Maria.

Rhea looked down at her empty hands, then back at the clock, which Maria had closed behind them. "Where's Sylvie?"

Without taking her eyes off the clock wife, Maria said, "She's in the kitchen, of course."

"Not *that* Sylvie." Rhea put her hands on the clock's case, but the glass was as cold and solid as ever. "The one in the clock, she was right with us. I thought I brought her out with me—Maria, she's been trapped in the clock!"

Maria did look over then. *"What?"*

"She said you sent her in—she said part of her left, but part of her was still in there."

For the first time since Rhea had met her, Maria suddenly looked old. Her face went slack and ashy. "In the clock? Part of her is still in the clock?"

She didn't know, Rhea thought.

It seemed wrong to feel such intense relief when Maria looked as if she had been dealt a mortal blow—and yet she did. *She didn't know. She might not have told me about sending Sylvie into the clock, but she didn't know part of her was stuck in there.*

There was a sound then—a sound she recognized. The front door was opening.

"No time," said Maria, pressing her wrist against her forehead. "No time. Years I've waited, and now I'm out of time . . ."

She squared her shoulders. "We'll set it right after," she said. "Come on. He has to have felt something happening, unless I miss my guess . . ."

Rhea looked down at herself, at the red dress, which had popped a half dozen seams, at the lump made by the pocket full of hedgehog. "I can't—"

"Go," Maria said and pushed her toward the door.

She went.

Ingeth was holding the front door open. Her eyes narrowed when she saw Rhea, and she made a sharp, impatient gesture.

But doesn't she see . . . ?

The clock wife walked a single pace behind Rhea, moving in her shadow. She should not have been invisible—she was nearly seven feet tall, for the love of the Lady of Stones—and yet Ingeth was looking only at Rhea and did not even seem to notice the figure that walked behind her.

It's some trick she's doing. It must be. Or something Maria's doing. She's right there. Ingeth should be running—raising the alarm . . .

Ingeth scowled, but that was all.

Rhea walked through the door and out into the courtyard.

The light seemed terribly bright after the washed-out gray of the beach inside the clock. There were perhaps fifteen or twenty people there, standing in awkward little clumps. An enormous crowd to her eyes, which had been looking at the same handful of women day after day for . . . for however long it had been.

She walked toward them, keeping her pace measured, trying to remember other weddings she had seen. There should be music playing, shouldn't there? Something to set the tempo? Someone on the flute or the tambour, someone playing pipes or a fiddle . . .

But there was no music. Perhaps Crevan had not thought far enough ahead to arrange for it.

As many times as he's been married, you'd think he'd be better at it . . .

Rhea had an urge to stare at her feet. Brides did not stare at their feet, did they? She looked up instead, at the people who had gathered to witness her wedding.

There was the viscount, whom she recognized from the midwinter feast—a big, round-bellied man going gray at the temples. His friend was marrying a peasant under his rule, and so he could hardly fail to appear, but he looked bored, and the people clustered around him seemed anxious.

When he saw her, he smiled, and Rhea had time to think, *Is he being kind? Does he not see what a wreck my dress is?*

She turned her face to the other side of the aisle, and there were her parents.

Her mother clutched her father's hand and took a half step forward, but Rhea shook her head minutely. *Not now. Wait.*

It was hard to walk by them, hard to see them slide out of her line of vision. *Soon. Soon it'll be over. One way or the other.*

Lady of Stones, if I'm going to die, please let them not be watching.

And there was the priest, standing under the metal arch. The golem birds had been taken down, Rhea saw.

Well, they could hardly be called festive.

All the people looked at her, and none of them looked at the clock wife.

Except for one.

Crevan stood beside the priest, half turned so he could watch her approach. She saw him blinking, as if there were something in his eyes that he was trying to clear away.

He almost sees her. He knows something's going on, but he can't do anything, not with the viscount right here.

People will forgive you for arranging a hasty marriage to an unworthy peasant girl, but they won't forgive you for making a public scene.

Crevan tried. He took a half step toward her, one hand going to his head, and his mouth opened and closed, as if he were trying to think of something to say.

She hurried her steps. There was undoubtedly some magic he could do—set the house on fire, summon an earthquake, make the priest fall down in a fit—something that would stop the wedding and leave him looking blameless. She could not give him time to do any of those things.

"Ah," said the priest, when she was only a few steps away. "Ah, yes." He swallowed, and Rhea watched his Adam's apple bob up and down. She felt a brief pang of pity.

You are out of your depth, poor man. And something terrible is about to happen in front of you . . .

"Wait," said Crevan, almost soundlessly. She heard him, but she did not think anyone else did. He licked his lips and opened his mouth to try again.

"Well. If we are all here," began the priest.

"Yes," said the clock wife in a voice like a great bell tolling. "Yes, we are all here."

* * *

A little wave of murmurs washed through the crowd. "Who is she?" Rhea heard someone ask. "Where did she come from?"

"Magic," said someone else. "Hush!"

Crevan recoiled and raised his hands in front of him. His eyes were wide, the whites shocking against his skin, as if he were a frightened horse rearing.

The crowd saw his reaction, and the murmurs grew louder.

Rhea felt the clock wife behind her, hot as a bonfire, and it occurred to her that perhaps now would be a good time to get out of the way.

"I believe, milord, that you already have a wife," she said. "I'll leave you to her."

She took three steps forward, grabbed the priest's arm, and tugged him aside.

"What . . . ?" he said. "Who is this . . . ?"

"Lord Crevan's wife," said Rhea. "One of them anyway."

"But . . ."

"Hush."

"I now do not love you," said the clock wife, towering over Crevan. "I now say that we are no longer wed."

Crevan's eyes darted around her, seeking out the viscount. "I don't know this woman," he said. "Or . . . whatever she is—a demon—I don't know her."

The crowd moved backward as a group. The murmuring was louder now, filled with alarm. Rhea could see her mother trying to move through the knot of people and hoped that she would have the sense to stay back.

"You took my death from me," said the clock wife.

She reached for him with both hands. Heat shimmered off her skin, distorting the air around it. Through the haze, Crevan's face twisted with fear.

He put up his arms to ward her off, and she grabbed his wrist. Crevan screamed.

The sleeve of his coat burned to ash. He jerked away, clutching his arm to his chest, and brought his other hand down across the air as if it held a whip.

The air crackled. *Some sort of magic,* Rhea thought, *whatever he can muster. He can't very well choke* her.

Whatever he had done, it knocked the clock wife back a pace. A line opened across her face, the gray skin parting to reveal flesh as white and bloodless as a fish's.

A sound came from her throat that no human had ever made, that no human had the power to make. Rhea's ears rang with it, and the priest slapped his hands to the sides of his head to drown it out.

The clock wife's fist caught Crevan across the side of the head and drove him to his knees. White dust rose up in a cloud when he struck the ground.

She towered over him, her breath hissing like water striking molten metal. Her head nearly brushed the top of the iron archway as she stepped through it. If the golem birds had still been there, they probably would have burst into flame.

"End it," whispered Rhea. "End it. Please."

Someone brushed past her. Rhea flinched back, startled—*Amazing that I can still be startled after all this!*—and watched as a slender figure hurried toward the combatants.

It was Ingeth.

She could not speak, but she clapped her hands together. The clock wife turned her head.

"Another wife?" she asked. "He then was busy. But my quarrel is not with you."

Ingeth held up her arms, shaking her head. As Rhea watched in astonishment, the silent woman made shooing motions, as if she were driving chickens out of the garden.

Oh, Lady. Oh, Lady, if Ingeth actually manages to chase off the clock wife, I'm going to . . . I'm going to . . .

Going to die, probably. Crevan's not going to forgive this.

The crowd had knotted up around the viscount, whose face had gone slack with shock. Whatever he had been expecting from a sorcerer's wedding, it wasn't this.

The dust moved around Crevan, leaving white streaks on his wedding finery.

The clock wife laughed.

"We may relive this differently," she told Ingeth. "You someday may find a way to drive me off. But not from this place." And she turned away from Ingeth, returning her attention to Crevan.

He was trying to crawl away, awkwardly, his burned arm dangling useless at his side. When she moved toward him, he made another whipping gesture and cried out as she slapped his hand aside.

"Go back," he cried. "Go back! I command you!"

"You bought my death," said the clock wife, "but not my obedience." She raised her hands over her head.

Crevan lunged.

Not for the clock wife, but sideways, grabbing Ingeth and pulling her before him like a shield. The silent woman struggled, her eyes going wide, but Crevan held her fast.

The clock wife paused.

Rhea could just see Crevan's face from where she stood. His lips were moving, his eyes were closed.

He's doing something—calling on some magic. He's using Ingeth to buy himself some time.

Behind Crevan, the white road began to boil.

Is he doing that? Calling up one of his monsters to come to his aid?

Crevan moved backward, on his knees, dragging Ingeth with him. The clock wife stayed where she was, looking over his head at the faces in the billowing dust.

"Oh, saints," whispered the priest. "What are those things? The giant demon woman was bad enough, but those . . ."

The creatures of the white road were coming.

They came as a dust storm, as they had once before, their faces billowing like gauze in the wind. The road heaved, and at last, Crevan took his eyes off the clock wife and turned his head to look.

The creatures' hands reached out, catching at Crevan's clothes, stroking their claws over his hair, and Crevan screamed.

I guess he wasn't calling them up . . .

The clock wife tilted her head. "They then have a prior claim," she said. "I now will relinquish mine."

Crevan staggered to his feet and tried to run.

Ingeth stood in his way.

"Ingeth," he cried.

She shook her head, reached out, and wrapped her arms around him.

He was still fighting her embrace when the dust storm swept in and engulfed them both.

Chapter Twenty-Nine

Cleaning up everything afterward turned out to be easier than Rhea expected, thanks entirely to Maria.

She came out of the house, stomped up to the viscount, and introduced herself as a witch. "Pardon me, milord," she said. "I don't mean to be forward, but there's a great deal of work to be done here now, and it's no fit place for nonmagicky folk."

"Ah," said the viscount. "Yes. This is—ah—"

"Up to witch folk to clean up, not fit for lords," said Maria. "But, milord, this is very important, if you'll take a witch's advice . . ."

The viscount spread his hands.

"The road there. It should be safe and settled now, but I daresay most of your people will be afraid to follow it. You'd be doing them a great service, if you don't mind me saying, if you'd take them home. They'll be looking to you for guidance, milord."

The viscount looked over at the white road, which lay silent in the sunlight, and coughed. "Safe and settled, you say?"

Maria nodded. "There were demons on it, but they've taken their master and gone back to hell, begging your pardon for saying so about my betters, milord."

(Rhea rolled her eyes at this obsequiousness but was too busy holding her mother, who was sobbing quietly, to object.)

"But people less discerning than yourself, milord, might still be afraid of it. I'm afraid it's up to you to lead them and show them there's naught to fear, sir."

"Ah," said the viscount. "Um. Yes. Yes, I suppose that's . . . ah." He glanced around. "And Crevan . . . ?"

"Not my place to say, milord, but I'd not be looking for him to come back."

Perhaps it was the little magic left to Maria, or perhaps the viscount was growing increasingly uncomfortable with the notion that his friend and political ally had been trafficking with demons. It helped that the clock wife had vanished once more.

It probably also helped that some of the crowd had seen the dust demons get their claws into Crevan before they vanished.

At any rate, the viscount shook himself and ordered his lackeys to get their horses in order, and in a very short time, they were riding—very cautiously—down the white road and away. The priest was the last in the procession, and to Rhea's mind, he looked like a man who was very seriously considering another vocation.

Rhea took the opportunity to introduce her mother and father to the hedgehog. "This is my hedgehog. Um. Not like a pet. It's more like a friend."

"It's a familiar," said Maria, bustling up. And when Rhea turned and stared at her, she added, "What? You think normal hedgehogs act that way?"

"But I'm not a witch," said Rhea.

The hedgehog rolled its eyes.

"Not at the moment," said Maria. "Maybe not ever. But you might surprise yourself. Come back when you're a bit older, and I might be able to teach you a thing or two. Now then . . ."

They went inside the manor. Maria sat them all down in the kitchen and made tea. Rhea glanced at her mother and got a reassuring smile. Despite the fact that her mother could not possibly understand what was going on, the smile warmed her.

Her father looked completely lost and clung to his wife's hand.

"Where did the clock wife go?" asked Rhea. It occurred to her that she should probably be frightened, but she seemed to have used up all her fear, probably for the next fifty years. "I promised her—"

"A death," said Maria. "It's been taken care of."

"You mean Crevan?"

Maria snorted. "No. She relinquished her claim to him—you heard her. No, I gave her mine."

Rhea stared at her, her fingers locked around the mug. Her mother quietly fed raisins to the hedgehog.

"It was a perfectly good death," said Maria defensively. "I hadn't used it. She took it and went somewhere else. Some other time maybe. It's hard to tell with creatures like her."

"Does this mean you're not going to die?" asked Rhea.

"It might," said Maria. She dolloped honey into her own mug. "But I wasn't planning on dying anytime soon, so it works out for now. The nice thing about immortality is that you have plenty of time to figure out how to get rid of it. Don't worry about me."

She cleared her throat and glanced at Rhea's parents, who were still politely pretending that a terrifying conversation about magic was not going on at the same table. "You'll be going home with them, of course."

"Yes," said Rhea's mother. "She's coming home with us. Back to the mill."

"Is the viscount going to take it away from us?" asked Rhea. "I didn't want that—I know I probably embarrassed him."

"I wouldn't worry about that," said Maria. "If you have any trouble, I'll be here." She smiled faintly. "At least for the foreseeable future."

* * *

And then there was only one thing left to do.

Rhea convinced her mother, with difficulty, to stay behind at the manor. "It's nothing dangerous," she said. "It's just—I'll explain it all later. I promise I'll be back soon, and we'll all go home."

"If you're sure . . . ," said her mother, and the hedgehog rubbed its snout against her mother's hand and made her smile.

And so the three of them went down the forest path together, Maria, Rhea, and Sylvie, the last of Crevan's wives.

Sylvie's step was surer. Her sight had not returned—apparently Crevan's death had not cured that—but the part of her that had gone missing had come back with Rhea and the clock wife after all.

"There's no amount of apologies that'll make it up to you," said Maria bluntly as they walked. "I had no idea some of you was still in that clock."

"It's all right," said Sylvie, smiling. "I'm back now."

"You know you'll never need to worry about a home," said Maria. "As long as you can stand me, that is."

Sylvie laughed and clasped her hand.

When they reached the golem wife's pool, they stopped. Maria led Sylvie to a seat on one of the stones by the water, and Rhea took out her knife.

The two of them waded into the pool, over to where the golem wife hung.

"Is she—" Rhea began.

"Not yet." Maria shook her head. "I think she's hanging on out of habit."

Rhea took a deep breath.

"Her name was Hester."

"Hester," said Rhea quietly. "Hester, can you hear me?"

Slowly, so slowly, the dried leather eyelids slid open. The golem wife's fingers twitched.

"Crevan's dead," said Rhea. "You don't have to stay alive anymore, if you don't want to."

She glanced at Maria, and the witch nodded once.

The golem wife's lips cracked open.

"Ahhh . . . ," she whispered, and then she did not move again.

Rhea bowed her head.

A little time passed, and then Maria sighed. "All right. Let's cut her down."

Rhea cut the leather thongs with the knife, and Maria clasped the dried husk to her chest, and they lowered Hester's body into the pool.

"Should we bury her?" asked Rhea.

Maria shook her head. "She was thirsty for a long time," she said. "I think she might like to lie in the pool for now."

"All right."

They waded back to shore and left the golem wife lying in the water, her sunken face turned toward the sky.

Rhea pulled the silver ring off her finger and tossed it into the water. Maria smiled.

"That's the last of us, then," said Rhea. "Isn't it?"

Maria nodded. "The clock wife's . . . well, happy where she is, I suppose. If creatures like her are ever happy. And I'll take care of Sylvie."

"And I'll take care of you," said Sylvie.

Rhea laughed, then sobered. "And Ingeth . . . ?"

"Gone," said Maria shortly. "Gone beyond our ability to help."

Rhea scuffed at the moss with her foot.

Maria sighed. "At the end, she did the right thing," she said. "I can't say I loved her, but I'll let the last act pay for all."

"Do you think she's suffering?" asked Rhea.

Maria shook her head. "I don't know. I hope not."

"Crevan, though . . ." Rhea tried to remember the faces of the things on the white road, but they had been too dreamlike to pin down in memory. "They got him, didn't they?"

"Oh, aye," said Maria. "You make bargains with dark powers, and they always come back for you in the end. His were just waiting for an opening. If he comes back, it'll be as one of those things himself."

Rhea glanced at the witch. It occurred to her that if one were being uncharitable, Maria herself might count as a dark power that had come for Crevan in the end.

Maria cleared her throat. "You might want to keep it in mind. I meant it when I said that you should come back when you're a bit older. If you're witch enough to have a familiar, you're witch enough to get yourself into trouble. Might be I could help you with that."

"I want to go home," said Rhea. The hedgehog shifted in her pocket. "I want to go home and think about milling grain and not think at all about magic or marriage or any of this."

"Fair enough. But don't leave it too long."

They turned toward the entry to the clearing.

There was a dark shape sitting in it.

"Ah," said Maria before Rhea had a chance to be frightened. "So you found your way back, did you?"

The bear whuffed. It ambled toward the women, claws scraping on the white stones.

"Foolish old girl," said Maria, digging her fingers into the bear's ruff. "I missed you."

Rhea put her hand in her pocket and petted the hedgehog. Her familiar, apparently.

Well. I suppose it's not as impressive as a bear. A lot more portable, though.

"You'll come back to visit us, won't you?" asked Sylvie. "Not right away, maybe, but eventually?"

Rhea glanced over at the blind woman's earnest face, and then at Maria.

Maria stopped petting the bear long enough to spread her hands.

"Well," said Rhea. "Eventually. I suppose."

"That'll be all right, then," said Sylvie.

The hedgehog sighed and curled up in a ball, and the three of them began the long walk home.

Acknowledgments

Thanks on this one are tightly clustered, mostly to my editor Brooke Spangler (who endured more of the stones and arrows of outrageous fortune than any one person should) and my agent and the good people at 47North who made this book more than the original sum of its parts!

To my proofreaders, who saw this before anyone else—thank you.

To my faithful blog readers, who are awesome and who were enthusiastic about this when I wrote the first few lines eight years ago and continued to be enthusiastic when, in fits and starts, I came back and poked it again and again.

To the staff of the now-defunct Pittsboro General Store restaurant, where I would go in every day and order coffee and a chicken salad sandwich. The first half of this book was written there.

And to the staff of Cafe Diem, formerly Davenport, the coffee shop where I would go in and order coffee and more coffee and then slightly more coffee. The rest of this book was written there.

And finally, my thanks and all my love to my husband, Kevin. There is a place in everything I write, at about the three-quarter mark, where I lose all my confidence and force him to read what I have and tell me whether or not it will shame my ancestors. He has therefore endured more cliffhangers than any man should be forced to endure, as well as me hovering over him while he reads, going, "You twitched! What made you twitch? Was it a funny bit? Was it a bad bit? *Tell me, tell me, oh god, is it horrible?!*"

Despite this, he stays married to me. (I think it's because I buy him sushi.)

You are all the best sort of people, and I am flattered that you let me hang around with you.

About the Author

Photo © 2013 J. R. Blackwell

T. Kingfisher is the vaguely absurd pen name of an author from North Carolina. In another life, she writes children's books and weird comics and has won Nebula, Hugo, Alfie, Sequoyah, and Ursa Major awards, as well as a half dozen Junior Library Guild selections.

This is the name she uses when writing things for grown-ups.

When she is not writing, she is probably out in the garden, trying to make eye contact with butterflies. Learn more at www.tkingfisher.com.